The Terpsichore Project

By Jim Taylor

to Fred, a good dear friend
and comrade in arms,

Jim Taylor
'Max'

Fur Elise

Table of Contents

Chapter 1 - Castañeda Revisited

Today is the first day of the rest of your life. Yeah, it was that old cliché from the 1960's and Todd Jamison was trying to hold that thought as he sped down Interstate 55 in his well worn hatchback. He was leaving it all behind. No looking back, just trying to stay focused on the road ahead. An hour ago he left Memphis headed for New Orleans.

It was September 2006, barely a year after the tragedy of Hurricane Katrina. The plan was to arrive by day's end, find a cheap place to spend the night and prepare for a life changing meeting he had scheduled in the morning. Everything hinged on the outcome of that meeting. Should the meeting be a failure, there was no plan B. He simply was unwilling and unable to think beyond that.

By now he was clear of Memphis and its surrounding congestion. He reached into the glove compartment and located his favorite homemade CD. It was all songs he'd heard hundreds of times. As the music took its effect, he settled into a zone. The hatchback was running on cruise control now and his mind was following suit.

Then as he approached Clarksdale Mississippi, a road sign caught his attention. 'Delta Blues Museum Next Exit'. An impulse came over him. Why not take a side trip to the delta, the fabled, mysterious Mississippi Delta. Memphis might call itself the 'Home of the Blues' but the Delta was the land where it all began. It was the birthplace of the blues. All the founding fathers such as Charley Patton, Son House, Muddy Waters, Howlin' Wolf and the greatest of them all, Robert Johnson were from the Delta. Blues folklore had it that Johnson had gone to a secret magical crossroads and sold his soul in exchange for his otherwise inexplicable singing and guitar playing wizardry.

Todd considered the irony. Despite all the years living in Memphis so close to the Delta, he had never been there. He had read entire books about the musical and cultural significance of this region. But he had never set foot there.

There were legitimate reasons. He had always been too busy. There was work, family, in laws, endless home renovation projects and, last but not least, more work. In workload as in money, them that's got it tend to get more. Besides no one else shared or understood his interest. There's nothing down there, waste of time everyone told him. And the kicker, his wife didn't get it.

Well, that was all history now. After decades of slavish routine he was starting a new life. For everything there is a season. And now was the season of doing new things, of doing things for the first time. What better way to inaugurate this new phase of his life? And when might he pass this way again?

On the other hand, he really shouldn't. He had a lot of miles to cover and little time to spare. There was the all important meeting in the morning. It galled him to think he should have made this decision before now, before he had to leave Memphis. And that realization was enough to make him decide. It was the sentiment that had informed many a decision in his life. Fuck 'em if they can't take a joke, let's do this.

Too late. He had just passed the exit. Well damn! How did that happen? How long had he been mentally playing with himself while deliberating this decision? Rather than turn back he determined to take the next exit. It turned out to be 21 miles further south and went to someplace called Payce. Payce? One of those Mississippi names as people in Memphis liked to say. Small towns in the Delta were often named for the man who owned the biggest farm which was likely the case here.

Just off the exit, there was the usual gas station and convenience store and then, nothing. The well kept road ended a quarter of a mile from the interstate. At least it was paved, sort of. Seems the much touted Tunica casino money hadn't trickled down to this neck of the woods. He was obliged to slow down to 15 miles per hour. He had definitely succeeded in taking the proverbial 'road less travelled'. For a moment he thought of turning around. Then he put it out of his mind. No turning back; no looking back. This was no book. There were no museums or tourist attractions on this road. He was in the real Delta. This was perfect. Half convinced, he continued on.

At 15 miles per hour, he could get a good look at the countryside. The Delta landscape was flat and unlike anywhere else in the state. It was almost devoid of trees with vast fields whose acreage stretched to the horizon. The few trees that existed were broken and scraggly as though strong winds had stripped them of their limbs and foliage. To his blues challenged, nay saying friends, it might have seemed as bleak as the Dakotas. Yet Todd found it fascinating in its bleakness. It was at once pastoral and surreal. As he looked out at the unrelenting flat stretches, he lost all sense of time. He felt as though he might have been the only person for miles around.

By now, his misgivings had been thoroughly swept away. He scarcely felt the road bumps. The words he had read about the Delta became living things. His imagination flooded with ghosts of blues past. He could almost hear distant echoes of field hollers, playful bantering, sexual innuendos and even peccadilloes taking place in between rows of high cotton. Saying or doing anything to pass the time until Saturday. Then counting the hours and minutes until Saturday noon when the week's labors were ended. Saturday afternoons would be spent in the nearby town sitting on a bench and discussing, even bragging, about how one might spend the coming evening. Then came Saturday night and its often dangerous revelry that would provide respite to the harsh reality of truly living the blues. As the life of B. B. King exemplified, the book on 'work hard, play hard' was written in the Delta.

After a few miles, Todd's reverie was interrupted as he came upon a rusted metal sign that read Bogue Beulah River. The wooden bridge didn't look all that safe but at least it was a welcome indication that the road might actually lead somewhere rather than dead end in the middle of a field. The bridge protested but held as he crossed. For the next mile or so the road followed the bends of the swampy shallow river. This was interesting at first but got old fast. Like an old retired man, the Bogue Beulah had nowhere to go and nothing to do so it meandered without purpose across the landscape.

Then the road and the river parted and he drove into the town of Payce, or rather what was left of it. It was a post-cotton ghost town. The rusty water tank that now served as a giant trellis bore stark testimony to a bygone era. Old King Cotton had lost his crown and the agriculture that remained was highly mechanized.

The most prominent feature after the water tank was the tumble down cotton gin. Behind the gin was a long abandoned railroad spur that ran off into the horizon. There was a freight house and an elevated platform where bales of cotton would await being transported to Memphis and sold at auction.

Just past the gin was a row of boarded up storefronts. One of them was last used as a senior citizens center. Another had served as a Head Start program center. Both were now empty. There were a few large homes that might have belonged to the major planters, the gin owner and the banker. Surrounding the big houses were bungalows and shacks where employees of the former would have lived. There was a school building that would have housed all 12 grades.

The entire town seemed like an old black and white photograph, grainy and frozen in time. He continued down the main drag of Payce. As he approached the far end of town, he wondered 'did anyone live here'. The question was answered when he noticed a lone man sitting on a bench in front of an old style general store called 'Leland's Sundries'.

From all appearances Leland's was the only going concern in the entire town. It added to the remarkable 'frozen in time' illusion. Being located on the edge of town it was adjoined by fields that came right up to the store property. The store itself was a wood frame, tin roof structure with a covered front porch that ran the width of the building. The storefront would have been a picker's delight. It was covered in porcelain signs advertising such products as Ex Lax, Goody's headache powders, Garrett Snuff, and something called Zero Ten. There was a large hanging thermometer in the shape of a bottle of Royal Crown Cola. There was a screen door at the front entrance that declared 'Colonial is good bread'. Yet another sign hung from inside the door that stated 'We Close Noon Thursday'. There was a single car parked out front, a vintage 1966 Corvette.

Todd just had to stop and get a closer look. He still had plenty of gas, good thing as it turned out, but he could always use a coke and a rest stop. Since he wasn't getting gas, he parked a polite distance from the front door. As he came closer, two rusted gas pumps in front of the store caught his attention. Obviously they hadn't been used in years. The registers would only go to 99.9 cents per gallon. There were handwritten cardboard signs taped to each register that stated 'pay twice amount shown'. Even with that the maximum rate would be limited to 2 dollars per gallon. This was 2006. When was the last time gas was that cheap? Was he in a time warp? On either side of the entrance were two wooden church pews that served as benches where paying customers could take a load off and have a good visit.

And there he was, the lone old man. He was sitting at the far end of the bench on the left staring off into the fields. As Todd studied the elder, he began to get a strange premonition. The man's posture was erect. His build might have been that of a man in middle age. But his face looked a hundred years old. Before Todd could look away the elder turned and caught him dead in the eye. Todd froze, then recoiled as he felt a physical shock flash through him. He managed to nod and offer some word of greeting but the old man continued to glare. Todd could now see that the man appeared to be Latino.

'Hola Señor?' he tried. Still no response. When the elder at last looked away, Todd retreated into the store.

Just inside, the storekeeper was sitting behind the counter perched on a captain's chair stool. Todd guessed the storekeeper to be about his own age.

'Well that was fair to middlin' awkward. And you handled it so well.'

The storekeeper had witnessed the entire episode and seemed amused by it. The good natured slight actually made Todd relax a bit. At least now he was in familiar territory.

'Yeah, kinda what I'm good at. Just thought I'd stop here and get me a cold drink.'

'Help yourself,' the storekeeper replied pointing to the old metal drink box against the wall.

Todd walked across the oiled wood floor and pulled open the lid.

What he saw was the inside of a true country store drink box. It seemed to contain at least one of every soft drink in existence. Overwhelmed by all the selection, he narrowed it down to root beer. Of the several brands, he chose a Frosty. He took a sip and cleared his throat. He was still feeling unsettled.

'If you don't mind me asking, what's up with that old dude out front? He gave me some kind of mean scary look. And when I spoke he just sat there. Did I do anything to offend him?'

The storekeeper stood up, offered his hand.

'Greetings neighbor, I'm Leland Everett, the proprietor here. I'm sorry; I didn't catch your name.'

'Uh, Todd Jamison. Pardon my manners. It's just that old man kind of weirded me out.'

'Yeah well, that'll be a dollar even for the Frosty'.

Todd fumbled with his wallet and paid.

Leland continued. 'Okay then, you would be referring to the Old Señor out there. That's what I call him. Weirded you out did he?'

Todd would have answered the rhetorical question but Leland cut him off.

'Now, not to be cavalier, but here in the Delta we're kinda accepting of weird. More than the rest of the state anyway. We believe in working hard and playing hard. We try to live and let live. Shoot, he's harmless enough. Nobody's ever been bothered by him, at least not until you. Most people don't even notice him. Those that do feel sorry for him.'

'Believe me; just now there was nothing about him that merits

pity.'
'Yeah well, having said all that, he is a might curious. I'll give you that.'

Just then Todd felt the urge.

'You don't have a bathroom do you?'

Leland pointed to the open back door.

'Neighbor, you got 6000 acres of soybeans and a big Sycamore tree out there. Anywhere will be fine.'

Todd was desperate enough to take this tongue in cheek response at face value and excused himself. Leland stopped him.

'No, I'm just messing with you. It's through that door that says employees only.'

When Todd returned, Leland continued where he had left off.

'As I was saying, he is a might curious. Nobody knows anything about him. He just showed up one day. I came in early to open up like I always do and there he was sitting out front at the far end of the left bench. I figured he was waiting on someone to pick him up but there he sits. And it's not like we're unaccustomed to Latinos you understand. They come through all the time looking for work. But they're young. This Señor looks ancient. No food stamps, no welfare check, no means of support. Never says a word. I'm guessing he doesn't speak English. All day he sits on that bench and stares out at the fields. He's there when I open at 6:00 am and he's still there until I close up at 6:00 pm. Where he sleeps is anybody's guess. For all I know he might just spend his nights on that bench. Might be he's got him a crash pad down in the old gin.'

Todd had read about yogis and mystics who could sit immobile for hours or days with little or no food.

'You said he has no means of support so how does he eat, or does he?'

'Not much he doesn't. People offer him handouts. But he refuses. So push comes to shove, I take care of him. He never panhandles. In fact, he's never said a word to me in any language. But there's something about him that just tells me I'm supposed to. It's like he adopted me as his benefactor. I'm happy to do it. And at the same time I'm kind of afraid not to. I never give him money. When he's hungry he just comes in the store and picks out what he wants. He always takes the same thing, jerky and a Nehi. I used to offer him a moon pie or a goo goo cluster but he never wants anything sweet other than the Nehi of course. Sometimes he takes a bottle of hot sauce. But not the Mexican, he prefers the Louisiana kind.

'He seems kinda religious. He might even be some kind of priest. Before he eats he always says some kind of chant. It's the only time I ever hear him speak. I guess he's saying the blessing. Sometimes I think he's talking to his food, apologizing to it.'

Todd sipped at his root beer and listened. Which was good, Leland wanted to talk.

'And it's not like he's gonna bankrupt me you understand. I own that bean field you almost peed in. Don't actually work it. I lease it out to a mid-western agricultural conglomerate. So technically they're sharecroppers. Ain't that a hoot? I live in Clarksdale. The drive backwards and forwards keeps the old corvette running good. And week end trips to Tunica keep the missus happy. This store is a family business started by my grandfather. Got him through the great depression. Now it's a family tradition more than anything else. Something to do. Entertainment value if you will.'

'Entertainment value? Really?'

'Oh yeah. You see there's more people who come through these parts than you might imagine. You just caught us on a slow day. I get a few people who took a wrong turn and got lost, like you I'm guessing. But the real action is the blues tourists. I'm an official stop on the Delta Blues Trail. I get referrals from the museum in Clarksdale. You wouldn't believe it. They come in here with their weird hair and their old beat up guitars speaking in British accents and French accents and I don't know what all. You never know who is gonna come through that Colonial bread screen door. The only predictable thing is they're always white and they always ask about the crossroads where Robert Johnson made his deal with Scratch or Papa Legba or some such. So I'll tell them a good story and they hang on every word I say.'

'Now that I can believe,' Todd thought.

'Then they want me to take their picture out in front of the store. I'll wager that there's photos of Leland's Sundries hanging on the walls of man caves all over the world. Sometimes I feel like this old family store is the center of the universe. I wouldn't be surprised if someday Keith Richards shows up wanting to buy some rinds and an RC. You know he did get busted a while back just over the river in Arkansas.'

Todd finally got a word in.

'Yeah, that's really cool. But we were talking about the Old Señor, as you call him. Tell me some more about him.'

Leland paused for a moment.

‘You really are freaked out about him aren't you?’
‘You should have seen the look he gave me. It went right through me. Then I tried to talk to him but he just sat there. I can’t explain it but he got inside my head. There’s no way I can just walk away. I've got to face him, make some kind of amends or it'll haunt me forever.’

‘Okay. I don’t know if this will help, but if it’s that big a deal, a small offering might be appreciated.’

‘But you said he never accepts handouts, right?’

‘Yeah, that’s right. He never accepts handouts. But I feel like I’ve gotten to know him a little. I’m thinking it's important that you do it as an offering or a tribute, not a handout. Somehow he’ll know the difference. Just saying. Hey I’m just making this shit up as I go. All he can do is refuse, right? It’s totally up to you, man.’

Todd thought for a moment.

‘Okay. It’s worth a shot. For all we know he could be this Papa Legba you speak of.’

‘For all we know neighbor. One more piece of advice. Don’t over do it. Ten is fine. And not to belabor the point, but if he thinks you’re doing it out of charity, something tells me that would just offend him all over again.’

‘And you’re just making this up as you go?’

‘Yeah well, that’s what I’m good at. Hey, you sure you got a ten?’

Todd stopped and checked his wallet. He cleared his throat.

‘Uh, I don’t suppose you could you break a twenty?’

‘Can do neighbor.’

As Todd nervously walked away. Leland offered a parting comment.

‘Hey, hoddy toddy. Johnny Vaught forever.’

Pausing at the door, Todd took a ten dollar bill and discretely palmed it. He turned back to Leland one last time.

‘Hoddy toddy. Thanks.’

Out front he struggled to face the Old Señor. He made his offering. The elder gave it a look without any change in facial expression. Todd waited a few moments. Just as he was about to turn and leave, the elder took it and tucked it into the breast pocket of his denim jacket. Raising the brim of his rancher’s cut straw hat he spoke, in perfect English.

‘I accept your gift because it is true. Gracias.’

Stunned, Todd somehow found the wherewithal to speak.

‘De nada. Uh you’re welcome. While ago, you looked at me like I had done something to offend you. I’m sorry if I did.’

The elder studied Todd for a moment then shrugged his shoulders.

‘I looked at you because I saw something. Perhaps when you looked at me, you saw something. Something the others don’t or can’t see. All they see is some strange old man, some homeless weirdo who sits here day after day.’

The elder closed his eyes. He took in a deep satisfying breath. Then he let it out as though all the joy in life were contained in the

simple act of breathing.
'All my life I have worked hard, in fields such as these. I am tired. You are not a young man. But compared to me you are still a boy. Should you live so long, the day will come when you are tired deep down in your bones. Then you will understand how blessed it is simply to sit and to breathe. For me every day is Saturday afternoon. Here, I have paradise and lunch.'

Placing his hand over his breast pocket, he continued.

'You expect nothing in return for this gift. That is good, for I have nothing. But I will offer these words.'

He looked Todd in the face for a few moments.

'You saw knowledge. That is what disturbed you. It is a fearful thing, knowledge. It is not something for wimps.

'A long journey brought me here, to my spot. I didn't seek it. My path led me to it. When I looked at you I could see that you are on a journey as well, not a trip but a true journey.

'You have lost your heart. You are on a journey to get it back. That also disturbs you, and well it should. You are ill prepared. Maybe you seek things. If so that is a mistake. Things are dangerous distractions.'

The elder continued.

'But you have chosen a path and that much is good. You must always seek to stay your path. It is not all laid out for you. Sometimes you have to feel your way. Make your fear your ally, as a warrior would. Walk your path with heart and your heart will find you.'

To Todd these words were at once gibberish and immensely

powerful. One thing hit home though. He'd lost his heart all right. This ancient shaman or whoever he was had gotten right into his head. How does he know this stuff? What is he even talking about?

The elder shook his head.

'You are full of questions that you can't even ask. And even if you could, there would be no answers. I'm all talked out anyways. You should walk your path now. That is where the answers lie.'

Then he looked out into the fields and became impassive. And with that Todd realized his impromptu tour of the Delta was over. After all, he did have a schedule to keep. He checked his watch. He could still make it to New Orleans by nightfall. He gave the elder a final nod and returned to the car.

Leland had told him that there were two ways back to the interstate, forwards and backwards. That was helpful. His head was already swimming from what all the Old Señor had said. Todd decided to continue on through town. He hated to backtrack. Besides, he reasoned, that would be deviating from his path. After 45 minutes and a couple of lucky guesses he encountered a sign pointing back to the interstate. At that moment he understood something as though some question had just been answered. Maybe there was something to this path stuff the elder had talked about. And just maybe his spot was out there somewhere.

Chapter 2 - Age, Attitude and Hurricane Katrina

After a minute on the interstate Todd set the cruise control. As he settled into a zone, the mile markers began to click by with agreeable regularity. He tried to resist the temptation to look back on his life. Too much lay ahead. Gone forever were the years of routine he'd known. For the next several weeks or months, he would be engaging an onslaught of new activities, finding a job and a place to live, hopefully making friends. In short he was starting completely over. He would be making major life decisions on a scale not experienced since his early twenties. Only this time he was old enough to fully appreciate what he was doing. It was scary.

It was by a combination of age, attitude and Hurricane Katrina, that he found himself at this juncture. Six months earlier he and his wife parted company. It was not overly traumatic or nasty as divorces go. It helped that there were no children involved. No, it was more a case of 'cancelled due to lack of interest'. Even so, he pained at the memory of signing the papers and saying that final goodbye at the attorney's office. All he could manage was a lame line from the Blues Brothers movie, 'see you around'. Somehow she was able to give it a laugh albeit a forced, strange laugh. Then she turned and walked away without looking back. She left town the next day. He sensed he would not see her again. It was one of those moments, the tragedy of which just washes over you. Like in a dream where you're drowning but still breathing. You should be feeling pain but instead you're just overwhelmed with a Novocaine numbness. The only thing missing was Barbra Streisand singing 'The Way We Were'.

But the next day the sun rises. You get up and go through the motions. You lose yourself in your daily routine. And the next thing you know it's six months later. And here you are, headed to

New Orleans, to a new job and a new life.

Oh yeah. Just two weeks after the divorce was finalized he lost his job. Did the divorce have anything to do with it or was it just a coincidence? He could be plenty paranoid. But he would never know. Don't take this personally they had told him. It was simply a business decision. In a way they were right. It was a common scenario these days. He was just another 50 something computer geek who never learned the handshake and thus became a corporate downsizing casualty. His 50th birthday just one week later had been a non event to say the least.

Todd realized he had lapsed into reverie. Enough of that. Tonight he would find a cheap motel room in New Orleans, clean himself up and prepare for the big meeting he had scheduled tomorrow. What the hell, it's only his life.

Chapter 3 - Teebow's Motor Court

A tank of gas and three rest stops later Todd was approaching the outskirts of New Orleans. It was 6pm and he felt tired. He got off the interstate at the Louis Armstrong International Airport exit. He drove along Veterans Boulevard through the city of Kenner and into the city of Metairie. Not finding anything that suited his mood or his budget, he turned right on to what looked like a promising street and headed south until it t-boned into Airline highway. He turned left and headed east. Crossing the Orleans Parish line he was now in the city limits of New Orleans. Here he found himself in an older part of town. Things looked more promising. The motels were non-chain, 'mom and pop' looking places. This one ought to do he thought. It's just for one night. So he turned into the driveway of a place called Teebow's Motor Court.

Teebow's sat on a small lot of concrete slabs. The only landscaping consisted of weeds that grew in the cracks between the slabs. The lodge itself was a squat 'L' shaped structure straight out of the 1950's. There were 12 rooms with the office located in the bend of the 'L'. Hidden from the front view was the manager's apartment that adjoined the office. He pulled under the drive thru, killed the engine and entered the office.

'Can I get a room for tonight?' he said to the person behind the desk.

She was middle aged but beyond that her age was impossible to guess. She had reddish, graying hair. She spoke with the unique New Orleans accent he had heard many times before on business trips.

‘Sure, we just had a vacancy free up,’ she said with sarcasm.

She looked him up and down thinking out loud.

‘You’re new in town. Not from here but you don’t look like a tourist either.’

Suddenly she changed gears and took the edge off with a smile.

‘Well, I think Teebow’s can accommodate you. Just the one night? You know, we have a special weekly rate. We’re actually a bed and breakfast. If you stay the week, I can feed you breakfast, no extra charge.’

She raised her eyebrows and gave an imploring look.

‘You look tired, Cher. And hungry. I’ll even feed you tonight. It’s not bad. My brother is a chef and brings by leftovers from his kitchen.’

She smiled agreeably. Truth be told she looked pretty tired herself but her eyes flashed with passion. Todd was caught off guard by her ‘not quite hitting on him’ sales pitch. But something about her easy familiarity was appealing. Perhaps this was his intended intro to the ‘Big Easy’.

‘Well, I am going to need somewhere to stay until I get settled into something permanent.’

He noticed there was a dining area that amounted to three tiny tables in a corner of the office.

‘And you’re right, I’m tired and I’m starved.’

Her smile broadened.

‘Okay, put me down for a week’.

And now she was all business.

‘That’s $350, Cher, cash, in advance. No refunds. But that’s for 7 days, you understand, not just 5. You’ll find that’s a very competitive rate. There’s an ATM behind you if you need it. I’ll even deduct the service charge from your bill.’

Todd nodded in compliance and took care of the finances.

‘Thank you Mr. Jamison,’ she said. ‘My name is Ramona Geracie, you can call me Ronnie. Your room is number 3. Here’s your key.’

‘Thank you, Ronnie. Actually, my name is Theodore which, for obvious reasons, I changed to Todd in like second grade. And I have no clue why I told you that.’

‘Maybe because I totally get it. Get yourself settled in Todd. Take your time. When you come back I’ll have you some authentic New Orleans supper ready.’

He took his room key and returned to the car and drove around to the front of his room door. He took care to park between the lines of ankle high weeds. Opening the rear hatch of his car, he stared at the select few belongings he had chosen to take with him. There was the guitar that belonged to his uncle, the duffle bag from his military stint, and the shaving kit which was a graduation gift from his grandmother. The memories flooded over him. He was drowning again. He tore himself away.

With a bit of persuasion he got the key to work and entered his room. For Todd, it was perfect. Lots of mom and pop charm. It reminded him of his aunt’s apartment back in Memphis. There was a slight musty smell no amount of room freshener could hide.

He left the door open to see if that would help. The double size bed was well worn but clean. Same for the 1950's vintage bathroom. Black and white hex tile floor, pedestal sink, tub with an added on shower. Only the toilet looked out of place. It was an obvious replacement, nondescript but functional. It was all capped off with fancy boutique toiletries which was nice since he had failed to bring any of his own.

He ran the water for a couple of minutes to clear the pipes while he unpacked his bag. Remembering his appointment in the morning, he took care to hang his one suit in the closet to get out some of the wrinkles. Returning to the bathroom the running water had freshened some but was still lukewarm. After deciding that this was as fresh as the water would get, he splashed some on his face. Opening a packet of soap he washed the 'all day in a car' gunk from his pores and toweled off. He was low on toothpaste so instead of brushing his teeth he decided just to rinse the stale taste from his mouth. He left the room and again, with some persuasion, managed to get the door locked behind him.

As he entered the motel office he was overwhelmed by the smell of something delicious. Of the three tiny dining tables he chose the one with the two place settings. Ronnie came over with a covered soup tureen and set it on one of the adjoining tables. She left and returned with a bowl of steaming rice.

'I know you're hungry Cher, but don't touch it. We're gonna do this proper. I'll be right back.'

She returned with a tray containing an ornate cut glass decanter of green liquor and two matching goblets filled with crushed ice. She sprinkled a bit of sugar over the ice and poured just enough of the green liquor into the glasses to cover the ice. The ice quickly melted and settled into the liquor. The liquor itself became a green milky color. She sat down and began to explain something.

Her age was indeed an enigma. Up close, there were touches of innocence in the face that were offset by lines of world weariness. He could see a little girl when he looked into her eyes. She began to speak. Her words took on a ritualistic feel. She spoke as if the world depended on her saying it just so.

She began, 'New Orleans is famous for lots of things and one of them is fortune telling. I used to tell fortunes at bazaars and fundraisers. My Grand Meme claimed to be related to Marie LaVeau. She said I had the gift and she taught me some of the finer points. So I'm going to welcome you to New Orleans by telling your fortune.'

Todd was puzzled.

'Wait a minute Marie LaVeau was African-American right?

'Well, you don't dispute Grand Meme's word. It's a long story Cher. Just hear me out.'

She took both his hands and closed her eyes. Todd felt a bit awkward but went with it. After a few seconds she let him go. Like a good fortune teller she began with the obvious.

'I can see you're new to New Orleans. I can tell you're looking for something here. Something more than just a living and a place to stay. The things you seek are good and true.'

Her voice became less formal.

'I can see you like us and our city. Lots of people don't. They don't get us. But if you truly like us, we will like you back. Don't take that for granted, Cher. New Orleans people, and I'm talking the ones who've been here a while, not the tourists, not the celebrities who've made us their latest third world pet. No I'm talking *l'anciennes*, the old time New Orleans people. They either like you or they don't. If they like you they will give you the shirt off their back, they will die for you, kill for you if it comes to that. But disrespect them, do them wrong and they're just liable to kill you. New Orleans people are easy going but I'm telling you, don't ever make a New Orleans person mad, cause when they get mad they stay mad. Okay, I might be exaggerating a little bit to make a point. But that's the kind of passion we have for life, for people. And that's the kind of people you want for your friends. If you want to make it here, seek these people out and avoid all the phonies. Otherwise the joys of this town, the blessings of life, will elude you. Show everyone and everything respect and you will have nothing to fear.

'Life is like a perfect brewed cup of French roast. And it don't matter if you end up in the grandest mansion on St Charles Avenue or a mom and pop motel on Airline highway. Every drop, every moment of life is full to the brim with flavor.

'I'm telling you things a lot of people don't know or can't appreciate. A lot of new people been coming in to town since the storm. They're all looking for something. They don't have a clue what kind of place this is or what they're doing. But you, you're different. Something made you decide to stop here instead of one of those chain ass places up at Fat City. That's a good start. I believe you're good people, Cher, not one of those phonies. That's why I'm telling you these things. You remember these things and you will find your home, your spot. Okay, the fortune telling is over.'

She raised one of the glasses, 'This is absinthe. Down in the French Quarter tourists pay $150 a bottle for this stuff. In the restaurant at the Royal Sonesta Hotel, it's served all proper by a gentleman wearing white gloves for $50 a glass. But this, this here is my secret family recipe. It costs me $8 a bottle to make which is about 50 cents more than what a bottle of grain alcohol costs. My brother gets it for me wholesale. But people I know who've been drinking for a long time say mine is just as good as the fancy stuff.'

Then she gave him the glass and took the other.

'Drink up, Cher'.

'To our health?' he suggested.

'To much more than that,' she said with watery eyes, 'to this beautiful, tragic city.'

Glasses clinked and they took a sip. Wow!! Todd had tasted similar concoctions, Ouzo, Sambucca but never home brew absinthe. Even diluted by the melted ice it must have been 100 proof. He chased it down with a swallow of water. It wasn't bad and when the burn in his mouth and throat subsided, he took another sip. As his empty stomach soaked up the liquor, his mind tried to soak up all that she had said. Her words rang true like those of the Old Señor. Did she say something about finding my spot? Before he could think about it too much, Ronnie emptied her glass and proclaimed 'Let's eat some gumbo'.

That was more than enough to make Todd remember that he hadn't eaten since morning. He watched as she placed a bed of rice in each of their bowls then ladled some of the gumbo over the rice. From that point, her persona changed from fortune teller to that of a mid-life widow who too often ate alone.

After devouring three bowls of the best gumbo he had ever tasted Todd spent the rest of the evening acquiring a taste for absinthe and listening to Ronnie's life story. He learned how the name Teebow's came about and what happened to 'pop' of the mom and pop establishment. She told him she had never remarried. She spoke of her large family, half who lived in New Orleans and half who lived in the bayou country. She remained close to her family but valued her independence as well. For years she had run the business alone with some help from her brother who was a chef at a well established restaurant. Todd listened with unaccustomed focus and clarity. Something in the absinthe perhaps or maybe Ronnie just told a good story. After she was talked out, she showed interest in his story and so he told her some about the life events that had brought him to this point. She teared up when he told her about the divorce. When next he got to a good quitting place he decided to excuse himself. She agreed. Big day tomorrow.

Chapter 4 - Sal LeBlanc

The next morning, Todd awoke at 6:58 am exactly 2 minutes before the alarm could sound. He was wide awake and felt remarkably good after such a long day before, maybe too good. His mind was racing out of control in anticipation of the day's activities. He got up and tried to calm his mind by focusing on the mundane, requisite bathroom activities at hand. Todd had a 10:00 am meeting at 1450 Calliope St. with some local honcho named Sal LeBlanc.

Sal LeBlanc was a recently appointed FEMA bureaucrat. Sal's office served as the Terpsichore Project Headquarters. Confusingly enough it was not located on Terpsichore St. but at 1450 Calliope St. in a restored boarding house. Sal had been given the entire building. His official title was District FEMA director. He was charged with repopulating an easily ignored area between the Central City and the Garden District. In an attempt to dress things up, the chamber of commerce had designated it as the Lower Garden District. Most locals still considered it to be part of Central City. The Lower Garden had chronic image problems.

Prior to Katrina, the Lower Garden consisted largely of commercial properties. Residential structures remained but they had been converted into either businesses or multi-family dwellings. Classic New Orleans style shotgun houses were the most prevalent. There were also two story town houses interspersed throughout. A few mansions still stood, from force of habit as much as anything else. The problem was that even pre-Katrina it wasn't particularly desirable. And it couldn't all be blamed on image. Much of the rental property was low income. It wasn't unusual for tenants to have a pig or a few chickens or even a catfish pond in their backyard. The barnyard smell could get pretty rank on a hot humid day, which is to say pretty much everyday. Although such practices were clear zoning violations, the landlords didn't want it enforced since the resulting evictions would hurt their occupancy rates. In short, Sal had been charged with attracting residents to one of the city's least attractive neighborhoods.

Sal's supervisor was Wiltz 'Huey' Fitzhugh, the FEMA Metro Director. They were long time acquaintances. Huey in turn reported to the FEMA Regional director in Houston Texas. Above that the 'official' chain of command led to Washington D.C. However there was an unofficial 'dotted' line that connected Huey and Sal with the so called local interests. And the interests had made it clear that as far as they were concerned that line was not a dotted one. It has been said that no man can serve two masters, but to politicians and bureaucrats in the Big Easy it was a way of life.

As if that weren't enough already, the fact that Sal and Huey had known each other for many years often made for strained relations. As an example, Sal's official job description was over 50 pages of federal agency legalese. Huey's version, delivered face to face, had been somewhat more succinct and to the point.

1. We have more government money than we know what to do with. Do something with it. Use it or lose it. If you lose it, the interests will remember you for it.

2. Don't get caught doing anything illegal. If you get caught doing anything illegal, my fault, your fault, nobody's fault, you will take the fall.

3. Always protect the chain of command. To protect the chain of command is to protect yourself. If anyone up the chain of command gets caught in any improprieties, you,

my old friend, will take the fall.

4. Always remember, I'm here to help.

No big surprises really. Sal had been a public servant in the Big Easy for a good part of his adult life. It was pretty much the way things are. But still, working for FEMA was something new. There had never been this much outside money involved with so few restrictions. The problem is he didn't have any legitimate takers. He had a strong network of local contacts but that did not serve him well. Most local prospects had left town, for good. Those that remained had taken advantage of the buyer's market Katrina had created and snatched up properties in the more desirable neighborhoods. A handful of celebrities had moved in and taken the crème de la crème of the Garden District. And they were mostly absentee owners. That narrowed down his prospects to out-of-towners. He had no clue how to reach them. He had no expertise on how to network outside the city. What he did have was a huge office and a fat budget. What he did attract was highly skilled, professional panhandlers and scam artists. In the beginning he was sympathetic and gave grants to anyone with a decent hardship story. The other neighborhood directors soon followed Sal's lead. Use it or lose it was the thinking. But it didn't work out. Sooner or later they took their 'Katrina money' and fled to Texas or the Florida panhandle and partied it away.

At first the FEMA brass were fine with that. Katrina was more than a natural disaster, it was a political disaster. Government ineptitude was on full display. The higher ups were desperate for anything resembling a success story. At least they could make the case that money was being disbursed to those in need. On the surface it all looked good. Then some of the scam artists began to brag about the secret of their success to others. This did not sit well in the politically conservative Florida panhandle. It was featured on several local news outlets. The story got traction and spread rapidly. It was to be featured on a national news broadcast. It was at this point that the top FEMA management in D.C. found out. More desperate than ever, they asked the network to consider not airing the story.

At first the network scoffed at this request. Then one of their news consultants pointed out the bigger picture. Their coverage had cast residents of New Orleans as victims, victims not only of Katrina but also of a distracted, unresponsive government from the mayor's office all the way to the White House. It was a compelling narrative and had generated huge interest nationwide. Their ratings numbers were up. Exposing these scam artists would tend to discredit their coverage. Moreover it would give ammunition to their fair and balanced rival who had taken a different editorial stance. That got their attention. In the end it was decided that the story ran counter to the prevailing Katrina narrative. The story was killed and hapless FEMA, which had become known as the new 'F' word, finally caught a huge break.

Nevertheless the heat was on. Sal was getting no guidance from the higher ups other than the fact that they were not happy campers. Desperate times call for desperate measures so Sal did something a bureaucrat almost never does, he made some significant decisions. Following the suggestion of a friend in City Hall who was a chief advisor to the mayor, he engaged the services of a consultant. It was an Atlanta firm who specialized in gentrifying old neighborhoods.

Sal quickly learned that they knew their stuff. The first thing they did was convince Sal he needed a program. The next order of business was to give his program a catchy, hope filled name. What they came up with was: 'The Terpsichore Project, A New Dance for New Orleans'. Sal liked it. Terpsichore was the Greek goddess of dance as well as the name of a major street in the neighborhood. The consultants also recommended developing a web site to shop the Terpsichore Project out to prospective takers outside the metro area. After much scrutiny and bureaucratic throat clearing FEMA decided they were happy with Sal's initiative and gave it their approval. Sal's boss, Huey Fitzhugh, who at first had been nervous with the whole idea, tried to take the credit. Of course in the end D.C. took the credit. Sal could have cared less who got the credit so long as the heat was off his back. Response was slow at first but serious inquiries began to come in. Last week the first internet applicant was approved. They had a meeting scheduled today. He was some computer geek from Memphis named Todd Jamison.

Chapter 5 - Angst at 50

Todd's 6 month job search had ended 10 days ago on his computer with a hit on a intriguing website, something called the Terpsichore Project. It wasn't his first choice. It was rather an act of desperation. In Memphis he had sat for numerous interviews but with no call backs. When he would follow up he would be told that his skills were dated, which they weren't. It was merely code language for 'you're too old'. Either that or they were looking for someone with project management experience and he'd written computer code his whole career. He also learned that he had developed a reputation for having an 'attitude'. He just didn't 'walk the walk' or 'talk the talk'. He never learned the handshake. And the final straw, all the employment offices in town were swamped with unemployed baby boomers just like himself. After exhausting all his Memphis options, he realized he would need to be willing to relocate. He turned to the internet.

The Terpsichore Project was named for a street in the Lower Garden District. It was a FEMA sponsored program designed to attract residents to a stigmatized and depopulated New Orleans neighborhood. Some considered its strong financial incentives to be an act of desperation. With FEMA's deep pockets, it could afford to be. It provided guaranteed employment in the applicant's field of expertise. It provided a free residence. Such residences were unlivable due to Katrina but the program would pay 50 percent of restoration expenses with the condition that neighborhood design guidelines were adhered to. It would provide for a temporary residence until restoration was completed. This all appealed to Todd who had run out of options.

First there were his financial concerns. He had lost his job at a bad time due to the arrangements of the divorce. The guaranteed employment was hugely attractive.

But there was more. Since his earliest business trips he had found New Orleans to his liking. He would always be the one to volunteer to go there when his old job required it. His colleagues were more than willing to let him. They had the attitude that it was a good place to visit once or twice but not a good place to live. Todd didn't feel that way. He felt a certain kinship with the people he met there. They were easy going and plain spoken. They reminded him of the small town people he had known growing up. He often wondered how it would be to live there. To be sure Memphis was a fine old southern city and had a certain charm. But it wasn't New Orleans, not by a long shot.

Then there was the adventure of it all. The catastrophe that was Katrina had transformed New Orleans into a frontier. For the bold hearted, or slightly desperate, it was a wide open opportunity. Just the perfect antidote for his mid-life crisis. His interest grew as he made inquiries and delved into the particulars of the Terpsichore project. At some point he understood that this was his thing to do. It had better be. For a nerdy dude just turned 50, this was a huge commitment. Someday he would write a book titled 'Angst at 50'.

Chapter 6 - Murphy and Uncle Bubba

Meanwhile, Todd was preparing for the meeting of his life and had become absorbed into his bathroom ritual. Stepping out of the shower, he lathered up while his face was still wet. He didn't bother to dry off first. There was no one to fuss about dripping on the floor. Those days were long gone for better or worse. He took great care not to nick his face as he got after every last bit of stubble.

His 10:00 am meeting wasn't exactly unexplored territory. Over the past 6 months he had become accustomed to the nervous energy that accompanied getting ready for a job interview. It had been plenty awkward going through the motions of a fresh face college graduate at this point in his life but he managed. Despite this, today felt somehow different.

He squeezed the last bit of toothpaste from the tube and began to furiously brush his teeth.

The contacts he had over the telephone and the internet had all been encouraging. He had already been accepted into the program. It had all been ridiculously easy. Just get yourself down here they told him. It was a done deal.

He deliberated over the three neckties he had brought and selected the foulard. He tied a half Windsor, didn't like it and started over. After four attempts he was satisfied with the knot.

So why was there this peculiar knot in his stomach? For one thing, he was 400 miles from the friendly confines of his hometown Memphis. And then there was Murphy's law which states that if it can go wrong it will go wrong. Every human endeavor is affected by Murphy's law but, with the possible exception of plumbing, none more so than software design which was Todd's gig. In the past he had dealt with Murphy's law on an almost daily basis. So from past experience Todd knew that today's meeting would present ample opportunity for Murphy's Law to rear its ugly head.

But perhaps the major source of anxiety was that it seemed too good to be true. When something seems too good to be true it usually is. This was something known among the Jamison family as Uncle Bubba's law. Since childhood Todd could remember his uncle pontificating to that effect.

He put on his dated suit and attempted to smooth out some of the wrinkles. Should have had it dry cleaned before he left. And with that final thought he left his room. He decided to drop by the motel office for a quick with Ronnie. He made a polite refusal to have breakfast which nevertheless resulted in a swallowed whole beignet washed down with a cup of strong black coffee. Then a huge go cup of coffee, some driving directions and he was on his way.

Per Ronnie's directions he got back on Airline Highway heading east. He turned right onto Carrollton Ave. then left onto St. Charles Ave. If you're not sure where to turn she had said, just follow the streetcar line. Then one turn onto Calliope St and he was there. Not the quickest route but the easiest. He found number 1450 Calliope with no problem. It was next to a billboard that proclaimed, 'The Terpsichore Project - A New Dance for New Orleans'. It stood out as the only two story structure in a long line of squat store fronts. There were no parking accommodations so he settled on the least dangerous looking street space.

Terpsichore Headquarters backed up to an obtrusive elevated six lane highway which led to a bridge that crossed the Mississippi river. Aesthetically this was a major buzzkill, however the building itself was quite impressive. Originally a single family residence, the late nineteenth century Italianate mansion had fallen into disrepair. It had then been converted into a boarding house, fallen into further disrepair, and now served as the Terpsichore Project headquarters. Despite the indignities of time, the building retained a certain grace. Memphis had some grand Victorian mansions but he'd never seen anything this ornate. This was another world. This was New Orleans. The rooms were huge, the ceilings were high maybe 15 feet he estimated. The woodwork was lavish and overpowering, probably old growth cypress harvested from the nearby swamps. One of the large first floor rooms was handsomely appointed with wainscoting and chair rail. Possibly it was the original dining room. The director's office was located on the second floor. He ignored the elevator and took the mahogany staircase.

He found the door marked with a big brass plate that stated 'FEMA District Director'. At exactly 9:58 am he entered the reception area. Sal LeBlanc's office manager was Debbie Cirlot. After a brief exchange of pleasantries, she invited Todd to sit and entered Sal's office.

'There's a Mr. Jamison here to see you. He's not on the appointment schedule but if you remember we were expecting him. He's kinda nervous and spaced out.'

Sal nodded knowingly. He had left the Jamison appointment off the daily schedule on purpose. After Sal made a number of ill advised grants to scam artists who took the money and disappeared, FEMA management had gotten nervous. Grants were suspended in favor of a pay as you go procedure. Written reports of all financial transactions were now required. Of course this new policy was too much like work for FEMA so Sal's own office ended up furnishing the reports. I know. Go figure. Todd Jamison was the first applicant that had been accepted over the

Terpsichore Project website. He was the test balloon. So Sal decided to play it safe. He would first wait and see if this guy remotely resembled a success story. Until that happened Todd Jamison wouldn't exist as far as FEMA was concerned. Years of public service had taught Sal the fine art of drawing targets around bullet holes.

'Well, he showed up. There's that. You say he's nervous Debbie?'

'Yes sir. After he introduced himself, the next thing out of his mouth was 'where's the restrooms?' I guess I should get back and show him.'

'Yeh do that. And Debbie, see if you can't chat him up a bit. You know, calm him down. I'm a little nervous and spaced out myself. Send him in at a quarter after. Tell you what. Before you send him in, how about you excuse yourself and come give me your take on him.'

Sal reached into a desk drawer and eyed his flask of brandy. Too early for that he thought and took out a cigar instead. All FEMA offices were smoke free but he could still chew the heck out of it. Out-of-towners he said to himself shaking his head. He had little experience with them but had heard how they are pathologically on time. But this one has to be two minutes early yet. He gave the unlit cigar a good chomp. Then he took out the unofficial Jamison file he kept in his desk. The file contained first hand information Todd had entered over the internet. More importantly it also contained personnel records from Todd's former employer. To get these latter records, it had been necessary to first obtain Todd's consent. It was all paper copy. Nothing had been recorded into the project database. That would all be done in good time if and when this case panned out. Sal had ordered a top of the line heavy duty shredder in case it didn't. Overkill some might say, but he had learned that there's no such thing as overkill when it comes to covering your backside. Once again, he skimmed over the personnel notes: computer programmer, 25 years with the same company, strong technical skills, weak people skills, lacks management potential, competent but not ambitious, has some attitude on corporate policy issues. In short, a computer geek. It was the comment about attitude that most concerned him. Laying down the notes he chewed his cigar and looked at his watch. Oh well, moment of truth in about ten minutes.

After a much needed bathroom break Todd took a seat in one of the antique chairs in the reception room. For the next five minutes or so he and Debbie engaged in polite conversation. She had lived in New Orleans her whole life and was interested in learning about Memphis. She asked Todd if he knew Elvis. Todd had long since gotten used to being asked about Elvis whenever people found out he was from Memphis. This time he didn't mind. It helped him to relax. Like Ronnie, Debbie had that infectious lilting accent and that same 'not quite hitting on you' charm. They had even gotten on a first name basis. She had yet to call him Cher. He just realized he had already come to like being called that. Then as though responding to some private cue, Debbie was back to business.

'Mr. Leblanc wants to see me in his office. I'm sorry for the wait. Please excuse me.'

Debbie got up. As she turned to walk into Sal's office Todd couldn't help noticing that the view wasn't bad. Never mind that shit he said to himself. Focus dumb ass.

'So what's your take on this one? Who have we got this time?'

Debbie gave her report with computer precision.

‘His face is such an open book. I feel like I know him already. His resume says he’s 50 but he seems younger. He’s smart but kinda lacking in gumption. He’s reasonably handsome, I guess, but seems unsure of himself. In a word, clueless. I calmed him down some but he’s still kinda spaced out. Of course from our prior conversation we can infer that he pees a lot.’

‘Don’t we all? I’m that way you know. The doc says I have a slightly enlarged pros....’

‘Yes I remember your telling me that before, more than once even. But with him it’s something different, something more behavioral.’

‘You’re the psychology major. So what’s your bottom line on him?’

‘Well I know I said earlier that he was kinda uptight. But deep down he’s laid back. For what it’s worth I think he’s New Orleans, one of us.’

‘What are you talking? He’s an out-of-towner, right? Hey, are you blushing a little bit?’

She looked away then down at the carpet.

‘Just saying. Why don’t I send him in and you can decide for yourself.’

‘Yeah why don’t you do that.’

Debbie turned to go back to her desk. Before she could leave, Sal added, ‘Hey Debbie. I hear what you’re saying. Maybe you’re right. Maybe this one will work out, eh.

‘And Debbie thanks.’

After Todd entered Sal's office, Debbie slumped over and covered her face with her hands. Her cheeks felt hot. Sal was right, she was blushing. Hopefully, Todd hadn't noticed. Duh? Of course he hadn't noticed.

Chapter 7 – The Interview, Divorce and Colonoscopies

Todd entered on shaky knees. He hoped this meeting didn't take too long. He felt like he could probably pee again. Damn, Ronnie's coffee was strong. Why did he have to drink the whole go cup?

Before Todd could introduce himself, Sal stood and offered his hand. After a few minutes of chit chat, Sal brightened. This Jamison guy wasn't what he had expected. He seemed like a regular person as out-of-towners go. He didn't particularly seem like a computer geek.

On the other hand, Sal was pretty much what Todd had expected. He reminded Todd of a slimmed down version of Wolfman Jack. And he talked pure New Orleans.

Sal became less formal.

'Hey, no more of this Mr. LeBlanc stuff, call me Sal.'

'Sure Sal and you can call me Todd.'

'I was just going to have a pee. My doctor says I have a slightly enlarged prostate. You can come along if you like.'

Todd quietly sighed in relief, 'Uh, yeah don't mind if I do.'

'Good we can talk some business while we're at it. Speakin' of doctors, you ever have a colonoscopy? They are the pits. It's the prep that's the real killer.'

Todd was only too glad to reply, 'Yes I have. I had my first one this year in fact. About two weeks after my divorce.'

'Are you shittin' me? I'm going through a divorce as well. So which is worse?'

'Hard to say. They're pretty much the same.'

Sal laughed aloud.

'You must really be a glutton for punishment.'

'It was just a case of everything happening at once. The divorce happens. Then I turn 50 and since I lost my job I had 30 days before my health insurance expired. So I go ahead and get the procedure done. I know it sounds kinda complicated but I can flowchart it for you if you like.'

'That's all Greek to me. Suffice it to say a man's gotta do what a man's gotta do. Now that I can relate to.'

Interesting sequence Todd mused. He was going to like this guy. Sal certainly didn't seem like one of those phonies that Ronnie had warned him about. He was, if anything, a little too genuine.

Sal's 'private' facility was enormous. In the original floor plan, it been designed for use when entertaining large numbers of guests at banquets and balls. It was richly appointed with dark stained wood, brass plumbing, and porcelain fixtures. There were three wall mounted urinals that stood on a raised platform. It was necessary to literally step up to the urinal. They ran flush against the wall from the floor to about chest high. Impossible to miss, even for Todd. From neighboring urinals, Sal alluded to an old joke and commented, 'That water's cold.' Todd played along and responded, 'Yeah it's deep too.' Judging from Sal's reaction Todd had passed some test. After this moment of male bonding they discussed at some length the details of Todd's application and the conditions of its approval. Todd liked the way they did business in New Orleans. By the time they had returned to Sal's office it was all but a done deal. Just some forms to sign. Most of it was a review of what Todd already knew from studying the web site. There was one condition that had not been previously disclosed. There was a list of 'neighborhood approved' contractors for the renovation of his selected residence. Under the agreement he would need to use the companies on this list for the various renovation projects of his residence. No big deal. Beats taking pot luck from the yellow pages.

Then Debbie entered with the necessary forms and showed Todd to a private area where he could read everything over and complete them. Todd by nature was inclined to read every word. He had been told by his uncle that the 'large print giveth and the small print taketh away'. The whole process took about 45 minutes. When he had completed and signed the forms, he returned them to Debbie's desk in the reception area. She laid them in a careful stack on her desk.

'Mr. Leblanc wants to take you to lunch. I'll tell him you're done. This is a big deal by the way. He usually has lunch with professional associates only.'

Apparently 11:15 am was not too early to break for lunch in New Orleans. This was unexpected and well received. Sal seemed like someone who would know the best places to eat.

Sal emerged from his office and announced. 'Mr. Jamison and I are going to DelaCroix's for lunch. Oh, and Debbie, I'll be out the rest of the afternoon. We have some business in the neighborhood.'

'Very good sir. Shall I call ahead and make a reservation?'

'We don't need a reservation at DelaCroix's. But have the car brought around.'

Sal laid his well chewed cigar on Debbie's desk much to her displeasure and they left. Like clockwork, Sal's personal car was waiting when they walked out the front. Sal got in behind the wheel. Todd got in and they drove off.

Sal explained, 'In New Orleans most everyone who's anyone has a chauffeur. I could have had one but I prefer to drive. I'll tell you a little secret, I use to be a chauffeur myself. Drove some pretty big dogs around this town. I was good at it too. As you can see, it led to better things.'

'That's very interesting,' Todd replied. 'Did you work for a limousine service or were you self employed, maybe?'

Sal cleared his throat. 'Actually neither, I worked in house for a business organization.'

A brief pause and he added, 'We're gonna have some lunch. The place we're going is good. Not the best, but I wanted to stay in the neighborhood. After lunch I'll show you around and let you look at some of the available properties.'

Chapter 8 - Delacroix's

DelaCroix's was only a few blocks from Sal's office. They pulled into the parking lot and were greeted by a valet parking attendant. The parking lot was full, everything from luxury sedans to panel trucks. Inside the restaurant, they were greeted by a man at the door who shook hands with Sal. Obviously they knew each other well. Sal made quick introductions and soon a waiter appeared who also knew Sal personally. He led them through the main dining room into a smaller room in the back. Like the parking lot, Delacroix's was filled with a diversity of patrons. Business parties clad in jacket and tie suits sat table to table with contractors and construction workers in jeans and coveralls. Sal and Todd attracted scant attention. The other diners were all absorbed in food and conversation. Todd frequented all the better known restaurants in Memphis but this was different. Again Todd felt the weight of a major realization. This was New Orleans. He felt comfortable, almost at home.

That all changed when they entered the smaller dining room. Here the clientele was considerably less diverse. Most of the tables were occupied by people who looked and acted as though they had been a part of the city forever. Here he attracted attention and curious looks. The furnishings were more lavish and more attuned to creature comforts. Despite this, Todd felt less comfortable. He felt out of place.

But Sal was clearly in his element. He introduced Todd to the waiter.

'This is Gustav, Gus for short. He's been taking good care of me for a lot of years.'

Todd noticed the name Gus on the name tag on his crisp white shirt. After they were seated, ordering drinks was the next order of business.

‘I’ll have the usual,’ Sal said.

‘That will be a double Martell on the rocks for Mr. LeBlanc. And for you sir?’

Todd hesitated. Gus tried to be helpful.

‘You look like you might be a visitor to our fair city. How about a Sazerac or a milk punch to get you in the New Orleans mood?’

‘What’s in a sazerac?’ Todd asked.

‘Lots of good things,’ Gus explained, ‘but the kicker is a splash of our special absinthe.’

‘Okay, Absinthe is good,’ Todd said with a nod.

‘Sazerac it is then.’

Gus nodded in seeming approval and left.

There were several important acquaintances and political contacts here having lunch. Sal excused himself and got up to work the room leaving Todd nervous and alone. Shortly, another server appeared and filled their glasses with iced water. Todd was thirsty and took a big drink. The server promptly reappeared and refilled it. Another nervous sip, another refill. Todd found this bothersome but when he tried to politely refuse a refill, the server looked confused and offended. A truce was reached when Todd figured out that if he stopped drinking from the glass the server would stop refilling it.

After a few minutes, Sal had made his rounds and returned to the table. He sensed Todd's discomfort.

'Sorry to leave you hanging. Gotta keep all the contacts fresh.'

Gus arrived with the cocktails. At Sal's suggestion, Gus ordered food for both of them. The cocktail went down extremely well. The food arrived and was delicious but Todd couldn't relax. There was something unsettling about the mood of their private dining room. It was actually too cold. He was relieved when the meal was finished. It felt good now that they were getting down to business.

Chapter 9 - 1256 Terpsichore

The valet brought Sal's car around and off they drove straight into the eye of a fascinating old New Orleans neighborhood. Sal felt the best approach would be to begin with an orientation tour. Afterward he would show Todd the specific properties that were available. Sal fairly lectured as he plowed the streets. His past chauffeur skills were coming into full play. He might have been reading word for word from a tourist brochure except for the passion in his voice which made it sound more like a lecture. New Orleans was his town. He had never lived anywhere else, and now he was showing off one of the great loves of his life.

For years the neighborhood had been considered part of Central City but now was properly referred to as the Lower Garden District. The Lower Garden or LGD was old even by New Orleans standards. It was developed following The Louisiana Purchase in 1803 to accommodate the influx of Americans to the formerly French-held New Orleans. Indeed the land from which it was developed had been a French plantation. Thus it became one of New Orleans' earliest suburbs back when the city limits consisted of the French Quarter. A formal street plan was drawn up and the streets were named for the classical Greek muses such as Calliope, Melpomene, and of course, Terpsichore who was the muse of joyous dancing. The area flourished and by the time of the civil war it had become the site of some of the city's grandest mansions. Alas, the ravages of war as well as yankee vandalism severely damaged the neighborhood. After the war, the 'polite' money moved uptown along the new St. Charles Ave. trolley line. The LGD was left to the designs of carpet baggers, developers and other opportunists. This era of gradual decline continued into the 20th century. Most significantly, the 1950's saw the neighborhood gutted by the construction of a new bridge across the Mississippi with its congested complex of entry and exit ramps.

After private interests had done their worst, the LGD became a ripe target for a series of publicly funded programs. Deserted old homes were demolished and replaced by commercial structures. Others were converted into duplexes, quadplexes, boarding homes and apartment houses in order to provide affordable housing. Many of these properties were bought out or imminent domained to make room for businesses and low income tenants. Existing residents were displaced and obliged to move out. And all in the name of 'urban renewal'. Ironically or perhaps predictably, these programs ended up doing as much harm as good to the people they were intended to help. Of course, as usual, the developers, builders, and other local interests got theirs.

The final blow came in the years leading up to Katrina when an unprecedented development effort had been focused on newly reclaimed marsh land to the east. As a result of this massive undertaking, New Orleans almost doubled in area. Large portions of the population moved east. Older neighborhoods were vacated and forgotten. By then, the LGD was at best low income housing and at worst abandoned buildings occupied by squatters and the homeless. Some of the more enterprising tenants took to urban gardening and backyard animal husbandry to augment their existence.

Incredibly, throughout this decline, a handful of old time restaurants remained open and viable thanks to the fierce loyalty of their clientele. In addition, the proximity of the Central City business district provided a solid lunch time business for a number of 'greasy spoon' establishments. Of course in New Orleans these establishments were capable of producing exciting and tasty sustenance and often received glowing reviews from local food critics. Each day business managers as well as office workers and blue collar workers would walk past flophouses carefully stepping over strewn wine and liquor bottles to get to their favorite lunch time establishment. Throughout its decline, the LGD retained a certain diverse charm which Todd had witnessed at lunch that very day.

Katrina of course changed everything. All of the low income residents of the neighborhood had been relocated to Houston, Baton Rouge and other cities. Once settled, they had neither the means nor inclination to return. So here were all these unoccupied residences. True, they were in varying states of disrepair even discounting damage from Katrina. True, some were rather humble structures. Nevertheless they were architecturally significant. They were one of a kind residences. They were built of old growth cypress and hand crafted with forgotten techniques. Sal's animated tour lecture had now taken on the moral fervor of a full blown sermon. He even surprised himself and apologized for his long windedness.

'Hey sorry. Maybe I should get down out of this pulpit.'

'Not a problem, Sal. You remind me of my aunt when she would start going on about Memphis. I grew up listening to all that.'

Sal shrugged. 'Okay, I'll be brief. And so, irony of ironies. After all that, after all the ill done by equal measures of greed and good intentions, here we are trying to cure it with more of the same. Another 'urban renewal' program, you might say, known as The Terpsichore Project. Ain't we human beings funny creatures?'

Sal shook his head and laughed. Then he became more serious.

'But this is different. This is my program and I'm determined to make it work.'

Todd was caught up by Sal's passion. Sal was making him feel as if the entire success of the project rested on his shoulders. After two hours of touring and learning the history of the neighborhood, it was time to look at available residences. As it turned out, Todd didn't have a lot of input in the selection. Evidently he has missed this provision when reading over the application forms. The gentrification experts from Atlanta had devised a master plan that would first focus on resettling the residences on Terpsichore street which ran through the middle of the neighborhood. Hence the project's title. Their studies of similar efforts in Atlanta and other cities had shown that once a critical mass of residents was established, small neighborhood businesses would be attracted. Gentrification would then spread from the center outward. To accomplish this end, financial incentives were designed to encourage development along Terpsichore. So Sal only showed Terpsichore street properties. He explained that because of their location these properties were key to revitalizing the neighborhood. If Todd wanted to take advantage of the FEMA funding, the selection would have to be one of those. At least he was getting first pick.

As Sal drove down the street, Todd looked from side to side. Nothing looked right. For the past two hours he had been driving past empty commercial buildings, ridiculously huge mansions and rundown vernacular style shotgun houses. He felt overwhelmed by indecision. This wasn't going to be easy. He would just have to take his time in deciding.

And there it was.

They surely must have driven past it during Sal's lengthy travelogue but he hadn't noticed it before. Number 1256 Terpsichore was a uniquely New Orleans architectural style. It was a two story structure and had the long and narrow profile of a shotgun house with some nice additional touches. It was similar to the house next door but something about 1256 stood out. It was adorned with columns and ornamental iron. To Todd's taste, it was like the baby bear's chair, not too big, not too small but just right.

'Hey Sal, let's take a look at that one.'

Sal was a bit incredulous.

'You talking this one here? 1256 is it?

Todd nodded emphatically. Sal pulled over, thumbed through an accordion file and pulled out a folder.

'Okay, let's check the file on this one. We had an Atlanta consulting firm do fix up evaluations, case histories and title searches all the way back to the original owner if possible.

'Can you imagine, casing these houses one by one? Taking detailed notes on each one all day, day after day? It's why there's such a thing as consultants.'

'Yeah, sounds like real tedious bean counting stuff. Been there, done that myself. But I would expect they get paid pretty well for their time and trouble.'

'Hello!' Sal exclaimed with a laugh. 'Don't I know it. I'm signing the checks.'

After studying the folder for a while, he handed it over to Todd.

'This one's in pretty sad shape. Here, see for yourself.'

'I thought you said they all were.'

'This one's worse than most. I'm just giving you a heads up on what to expect when we go inside.'

'Ouch. It's not all that great from the outside. But it's a cool old New Orleans house. It's got potential.'

'Yeah well, as you can see, this one was converted to a duplex and then to a quadplex. The original floor plan was completely trashed. New doors were added in the back and new walls were added to create more, smaller rooms. Well, shall we?'

They exited the car. Sal acted as though he owned the place. He apparently had no concerns about leaving the car sticking out into the street. Not that there was much traffic. Before entering the house they checked out the yard. On the street's edge was an impressive live oak which Todd imagined had been here when the area was still a French plantation. Its roots had buckled the sidewalk. Todd got an eerie feeling as he stepped over the protruding roots. For all he knew it might have been a 'hanging tree' in centuries past. There was a rusty but ornate iron fence surrounding the front. The gate would still open with some effort. Some ancient flowering bushes competed for light with invasive vines.

'Watch out, some of that's poison ivy,' Sal warned.

Todd stood out front and took it all in. It was beginning to grow on him. The most interesting feature was the double-decker front porch. The shuttered windows on both stories were the same height as the door allowing the house to be completely opened up to the front porch when the weather was nice. Great house for a party. He recalled his grandmother's front porch where after a hard morning of cooking and housekeeping, she would relax in the afternoon with a glass of ice tea and a crossword puzzle. Mammy would have definitely liked this porch.

They walked around to the back yard. There were areas devoid of any vegetation and littered with debris. This indicated just how closely the edge of the flood waters had reached. Sal explained that the LGD had been spared the worst ravages of the flood. However, there were low areas where the water had reached a depth of several inches during the outage of the municipal pumping stations. Since the streets were constructed on elevated road beds, the lower areas were mostly away from the streets in people's backyards. The flood water contained toxins, hence the lack of vegetation. There was also a pool that still held about a foot of water. Todd noticed that half of the pool was rather ornate and edged with marble paving stones. The undecorated half had been dug out from the original doubling the pool's size. Sal explained that what was once an old decorative goldfish pool had very likely been expanded and converted into an aquaculture catfish pond. Such practices clearly were zoning violations but landlords were reluctant to do anything that might interrupt their cash flow from otherwise good tenants.

'The flood waters contained some pretty funky stuff. I doubt even catfish could live in that now. But depending on who you ask, those dead areas in back should be okay in anywhere from 6 months to a year. Weeds always find a way you know. In the meantime, just treat it like one of those places where your mother told you not to play.'

'Shouldn't be a problem. I never was much for yard work anyway.'

'Let's go back around front and see if this key works.'

The consultants had done their work well. After the thrill of walking up onto the porch and entering, a huge disappointment set in. The floor plan had been redesigned to make smaller rooms. The rooms were way small and cramped. It was made worse by the fact that the original eleven foot ceilings had been lowered to eight feet. The good news was the redesign had been done with cheap materials and wouldn't be hard to rip out. In fact the workmanship was so shoddy Todd felt he could have demolished it with his bare hands. The added walls were barely standing. In stark contrast to the poor quality of construction, the interior was neat and surprisingly clean. The previous tenants apparently had taken pride in their humble digs. There were no holes knocked in the walls no graffiti or other signs of vandalism or looting. There was no garbage or rotten food strewn around. Everything had been picked up and disposed of. It looked ready to be occupied now.

'Wow', Todd remarked, 'other than that mildew smell, this place is neat as a pin.'

'Yep, I'm as surprised as you are what with all the looting and vandalism that was going on. Give some credit to our law enforcement community. You know it took a few days, but we managed to get our act together. Not that you'd ever know from the media coverage. And this neighborhood has been locked down ever since. I've seen to that. No one has entered any of these properties with the exception of the consultant firm's case workers. And even they were accompanied by a security officer.'

'I've seen a lot of rental property in Memphis. I've lived in a lot. Never saw anything this well kept.'

'Kinda shoots the hell out of the 'pride of ownership' theory don't it. Well I say pride ain't got nothing to do with ownership. You either got it or you don't got it. I heard that a lot of the evacuees didn't want to leave. They had to be, shall we say, strongly encouraged by the authorities. This was their home. I don't know much but I do know how you can feel about home.'

'Tell me about it. I left home yesterday.'

Sal realized the full impact of his comment. ‘Sorry Todd. I wasn’t thinking.’

‘No problem Sal. I was just agreeing with you.’

Todd had almost said ‘forget about it’. Luckily he didn’t. While he wasn’t overly gifted with people skills, neither was he naive. He had read between the lines of some of Sal’s earlier comments. At some point he had begun to wonder if Sal was in some way beholden to the ‘the good old boys’ or whatever they were called here. Todd now realized that this was the source of his uneasiness at lunch.

Sal didn’t really seem like the type. No doubt he was a man who could do what a man’s gotta do. And yet his comments showed a sensitivity to the people of modest means who had lived here. Todd realized that underneath the impeccable hair and custom tailored suit was a complicated man with a good heart.

‘You know Todd, I’ve lived my whole life here in N'awlins. She’s the love of my life. So I can’t imagine what it’s been like for you. Having to pull up roots and leave it all behind. But we’re going to try to help you with that. You’re kinda lucky you know.’

Sal’s sympathy was unexpected. Todd felt tears starting to form and angrily fought them back.

‘Yeah. I know. I’m trying real hard not to fuck this up. Sorry for the language. It’s just that I’ve done my share of screwing things up lately. And after looking around the neighborhood all afternoon I now realize that it’s me who has no clue what all this has been like for you.’

Sal paused, maybe he choked a bit. Then he cleared his throat.

‘Me personally? I’m okay. A lot better than most. It’s been tough. But I’m in a position to help, not just you but this town. And that’s what I’m trying real hard not to fuck up.’

‘Okay, back to business. Have you got any questions or concerns?’

‘Yeah, how do I get started?’

‘You’re sure this sad little shack is what you want? There’s nicer and larger properties available.’

‘I know a little bit about fixing up old houses. I’m going to make this bitch the love of my life. All she needs is some TLC.’

Sal raised his eyebrows.

‘Okay. Good to hear that. First we’ve got some more forms for you to sign. Sorry about that; there’s boo coo red tape where FEMA is involved. You’ve had a pretty big day. So why don’t we call it a day. I’ll take you to your car. I know you feel like you’re sure about this but still it wouldn’t hurt to give it a good think overnight. I’ve had a lot of guys take the money and haul ass to Florida, not that you would. But it’s an important decision you’re making. If you’re still sure you want to do this tomorrow, Debbie will set you up with the necessary forms. So where are you staying tonight?’

‘A little mom and pop place out on Airline Highway. I’ve already paid a week in advance.‘

‘We can take care of that for you. If you like we can put you up someplace closer in. The Pontchartrain or the Prytania is nice. I know some people who run things there.’

‘Thanks no. I’m good. For the week anyway. But I might take a raincheck.'

'Everwhat,' Sal replied, 'We'll reimburse you of course'.

Todd had forgotten about how broke he was.

'I heard that. I can get a receipt where I'm staying and bring it in the morning.'

'I've got a better idea. What we'll do is give you a cash advance. I'll get Debbie to take care of that as well.'

As they drove back, Sal explained that yet another consulting firm, this one from New Orleans, would inspect Todd's property. It would recommend how best to restore the property true to its original state and write up an estimate on how much it would cost. These recommendations would be incorporated into a master restoration plan. Next the master plan would have to be reviewed and approved by the city inspector for adherence to building codes. The Lower Garden District neighborhood association would then review the plan for preservation concerns. Everything down to the color of the paint, type of roofing, type of wood and even brick mortar would be subjected to scrutiny. New Orleanians were always sticklers for historical preservation in the Garden District proper. And now, with all the FEMA money floating around, that interest was focused on the Lower Garden District as well. Todd would of course have input into the restoration provided it did not go against the neighborhood association guidelines. Once the master plan was approved, the actual work would be done by contracting firms that were on the neighborhood approved list. The talking point was that these firms were certified and approved to do work on residences of historical significance. Again Todd would have some input selecting the workmen so long as they were on the all important list.
When they arrived back at Sal's office Todd echoed that it had

indeed been a big day, and a good day. After the months of dead end job interviews this was a welcome experience. He followed Sal back to the office for a quick bathroom break. Then they had a polite argument over whose pleasure had been the greatest and parted company.

He began to navigate his way back uptown through the New Orleans traffic. Although he had a pretty good sense of direction, that didn't work in uptown New Orleans. All the streets were crescent shaped due to the fact that they followed the crescent of the Mississippi River. He decided to play it safe and slavishly drove back to Teebow's the way he came, following the streetcar tracks. Traffic was slow but he didn't mind. It gave him a chance to indulge in something he couldn't do this morning which was to admire all the old homes along St. Charles Ave. The late afternoon sun reflecting off their beveled glass door ways added to their grandeur.

In contrast to this stately backdrop was the human comedy of uptown during rush hour. There were honking horns, clanging streetcar bells, and screeching tires. Amazingly there were no fender benders, just incredible near misses. Equally amazing, there was no road rage. Instead there was a certain business as usual acceptance by the motorists, joggers, and the occasional cyclist. There was even a certain rhythm to it. It was a dance and Todd was digging it. Feeling moved to participate in the dance, he honked when the car in front of him was slow in responding to a green light. The car behind him promptly joined in. He suddenly became aware of his necktie. Taking both hands off the wheel he yanked the tie off in one deft move relishing the surge of freedom it gave him. Like Gauguin, he was going native. The dull heartache that was always in the background had left him. He felt as though he were truly breathing for the first time in weeks. Maybe this was a fool's paradise. Maybe Uncle Bubba was right. When things seem too good to be true they usually are. But for the moment he didn't care. He was remembering and feeling something that Ronnie told him last night; every moment of life is filled to the brim with flavor.

Chapter 10 - Segway's Pit Stop

Todd found his way back to the Teebow's Motor court. He parked in front of Room 3 taking care to position the car between the weeds that grew in the cracks of the concrete. He took his few remaining belongings into his room. It had been foolish to leave them in the car all day. He was lucky that his car hadn't been burglarized. He hadn't been left with that much after the divorce. Which was fine, he didn't want a lot of reminders. But the few items that he brought along had been chosen with great care.

He changed into jeans and a polo and flopped onto the bed. It felt delicious like the old feather bed that had belonged to his grandmother. He realized that if he laid there for long he would conk out and probably sleep straight through until morning. He checked with Ronnie to find a quick place for supper. Of course, she wanted to talk again but agreed that a short evening was what he needed. But he had to promise to have a proper breakfast in the morning. She told him of a convenience store just over the parish line in the city of Metairie that happened to serve one of the best Po Boys in the metro area.

The place was called Segway's Pit Stop and was less than a mile away. He had no trouble finding it. It turns out he had driven past there when he arrived the night before. He was low on gas and pulled in next to one of the pumps. Luckily it took credit cards. Ronnie had insisted on cash to pay for his room. That last ATM withdrawal had seriously depleted his bank balance. Sal had better come through with that advance in the morning. After gassing up he went inside to get a sandwich. He was immediately greeted with the heavenly aroma of atomized corn meal and cooking oil that resulted from skillful frying. The man behind the counter was named Ed and he was helpful, sort of.

‘What’s good here?’ Todd inquired.

‘Everything,’ Ed replied, ‘We have the best Po Boys in the state. People come here all the way from Baton Rouge to East New Orleans. Or they did before it got washed away. God bless ‘em.’

Todd nodded in respect. ‘Okay. My nose is telling me I gotta have something fried. I’ll take the oyster loaf. And make it the King Size, I’m pretty hungry.’

‘Ha, you better be. If you want something to drink, just help yourself to anything in the cooler. Be a few minutes on your sandwich. There’s a dozen phone orders ahead of you. That’s what you should do the next time. You can pick it up at our drive thru window.’

Ed handed the order to someone in the kitchen. Todd turned and went to the beer section of the cooler. Then he turned and looked back at Ed. ‘I’m new to New Orleans. What’s the good beer in these parts?’

‘Well I can’t speak for New Orleans but here in the city of Metairie you got three choices. You drink Jax, you drink Dixie or you’re a communist.’

Todd took Ed’s comment at face value missing the humor. ‘But you have lots of other brands.’

Ed was unflapped. ‘Hey, we get lots of communists in here. And mostly they come from New Orleans.’

This time Todd got it. ‘You know what, a six pack of Dixie sounds real good.’

‘Now you talking. I didn’t really think you were a communist.’

They shared a good laugh. Todd grabbed the six pack.

‘Man these are cold.’

‘Yeah well, here in the city of Metairie either you sell cold beer or...’

‘Or you’re a communist?’ Todd offered.

Ed had to laugh.

‘You know you’re kinda clueless but you catch on fast. Just saying. I’m a straight talking Cajun. Says what he means, means what he says. Everybody will tell you that.’

Todd relaxed a bit.

‘I’ll tell you something, I wouldn’t mind popping one of these Dixie’s right now. I have had one helluva day.’’

‘I heard that. But I’d advise against it friend. Metairie’s finest might not take kindly to someone with a Tennessee tag flaunting the law.’

‘How did you know I was from Tennessee?’

‘You talk funny. Just like folks from Tennessee who come down for the football games.’

‘So you’re a big LSU football fan I’m guessing?’
‘Do I look like a communist?’

Todd laughed again.

Presently the order was ready. Todd knew from experience that oyster Po Boys dripping with remoulade sauce are an especially messy delight. Grabbing a handful of extra napkins, he settled with Ed and returned to the car. Then remembering he was out of toothpaste, he ran back in. Hurriedly he made a selection, this time without asking Ed for a recommendation. After he paid, Ed stopped him.

'You're okay neighbor, for a Tennessee man. I need to level with you. When you swiped your credit card to pay for the gas, your address came up on the register screen. That's how I know you from Tennessee.'

Then before Todd could leave, 'You still talk funny though.'

Todd couldn't wait to suck down a cold beer and dive into that po' boy but took the time to smile and wave good bye.

Back at the motel he cleared off a makeshift dining area on the desk and dug in. Ed had been right; he could barely eat half the sandwich. He managed to drink 2 of the Dixie's before exhaustion hit him. All the nervous energy of the last 48 hours evaporated. All the weight of that nonstop onslaught was settling over him. Doing new stuff when you're accustomed to routine takes a lot out of you. Being 50 doesn't help either. Throwing his clothes on the back of the chair, he collapsed into the bed. Soon he was in a deep sleep. This was a blessing. No opportunity to think about being homesick. He awoke once, got up to pee and promptly went back to sleep.

Chapter 11 - Ed Segura

The next morning Todd awoke feeling rested. He had slept soundly. Then an 'oh shit' moment. Had he overslept? He checked his watch. It showed 6:58. He breathed a sigh of relief. Oversleeping was one of his recurrent nightmares. Then as his mind began to stir he remembered that his meeting with Sal today was not until 11:00 am. He breathed another sigh of relief. He was looking forward to a leisurely breakfast where he could drink a gallon of coffee and be close to a familiar bathroom. He shook his head. The things age does to your priorities.

Needing some caffeine now he threw on a pair of jeans and a pull over shirt. Then he went to the motel office to help himself to the coffee service Ronnie had put out earlier. The coffee was contained in a generous thermal carafe. He knew it would be good and strong. Ronnie told him that she always hand poured it twice through a drip style coffee maker. She had also put out a couple of generous sized stoneware mugs, no styrofoam cups in her establishment. What a jewel in the rough Teebow's had turned out to be. He poured himself a cup and returned to his room.

The next few minutes were spent savoring the coffee and feeling his head grow clearer. Having the luxury of some time to kill he pulled out the Gibson guitar that had belonged to his uncle and banged out a few tunes on it. It sounded good. He hadn't played it in a few days and he felt like being in New Orleans gave it a different sound, a New Orleans sound. An hour later he realized he should start getting ready for his day. After his usual bathroom ritual he decided to stick with the jeans. That seemed too casual so he added the jacket. He couldn't tell if it made things better or worse. Finally he just went with it.

When he returned to the motel office, Ronnie was still busy in the kitchenette adjoining the office.

'Good morning,' Todd announced. 'What's for breakfast?'

Ronnie emerged. The morning sun in her face showed her age. It made her look older than he had remembered the other night. Again he told himself that they were probably about the same age.

'The best breakfast in New Orleans, Cher. Better than any buffet you would've got up on Veterans boulevard. But you know that already. You better. Take a seat and I'll bring you some breakfast. Then you're going to tell me all about yesterday. Oh, help yourself if you need more coffee.'

Todd obliged, took a seat in the three table dining area and savored his second cup of the day.

Presently Ronnie returned with two plates of something that resembled grits and fried steak swimming in a plentiful pool of gravy.

'This is some leftover steak my brother brought me. He's a chef in a fancy restaurant. It's called grillades. I'm assuming you know what grits are. Does it suit you?'

Rather than answer, Todd had a polite taste and then dug in.

Ronnie took that as a yes and the stage was set for some serious breakfast conversation.

'So how was your supper last night? What did you have?'

From past visits, Todd knew that in New Orleans people loved to talk about food while they ate. And so did he.

'I got the oyster loaf, king size. I thought I was starved but could only eat half of it. But was it good. Haven't had oysters like that since the last time I was here.'

'You had the best oysters in the world. I could have guessed you got something fried. I can smell it on your clothes. Is that the same shirt you had on last night?'

'Yeah guess I ought to change it before I leave today, huh?'

'And don't leave those leftovers in your room, Cher. They'll go bad. Bring it to me before you leave today.'

'Yeah good tip. I'll do that.'

'So who waited on you at Segway's? Did you get to meet Ed Segura? He's the owner you know. '

'Yeah, I guess so. Anyway he said his name was Ed, interesting character. Let's see, he told me he was a Cajun. Then he said that in the city of Metairie people who didn't drink Dixie or Jax beer were considered to be communists. Then he pretty much said the same thing about people who weren't LSU fans. And he said he knew I was from Tennessee because I talk funny.'

Ronnie threw back her head and laughed so hard that she nearly fell out of her chair.

'That's Ed all right. Always pulling your leg. Except for the Cajun part. That much is the truth.'

Todd got up and poured himself a third cup of coffee.

'So why would he make mention of that? I thought just about everybody here were Cajuns.'

Ronnie shook her head.

‘Lots of people think that. That’s a big mistake Cher. There’s Cajuns all over southwest Louisiana. Some of them got French names, some of them got Spanish names like Ed. Here in New Orleans there’s plenty of people with French and Spanish names but true Cajuns are few and far between. That’s because when they arrived down here from Canada, they were considered to be immigrants. New Orleans wouldn’t have ‘em. So they ended up settling further west in the bayou country. Acadians are proud of their heritage and they can get pretty touchy about it. My mother’s family and my in laws are Acadian. So I know what I’m talking about.

‘I’ll tell you something else. There’s muckety mucks who look down their nose at us Cajuns. Then you got people who ain’t even Cajun proclaiming to be Cajun just to make a buck. Cajun music, Cajun dancing and Cajun food are big business with the tourists these days. Ain’t that a kick in the pants? But most are like Ed. They’re proud of it and don’t give a good damn who knows it. Just don’t go around assuming everybody in New Orleans is Cajun. Remember all that and you can save yourself a lot of grief.’

‘Another good tip, Ronnie. Thanks’

‘Of course. So tell me about your big meeting yesterday. How’d everything go?’

‘Well it went good. I found a place I like. It’s a good size not too big or too small. Maybe a bit big for just one person but maybe I won’t always be just one person.’

‘One thing at a time Cher. Don't get too far ahead of yourself. So where is your place located?’

‘It’s on Terpsichore street in a neighborhood called the Lower

Garden District.'

'Yeah I know the neighborhood. It's really just a part of Central City. Used to be a big hangout for drug users and wino's, excuse me, homeless people. But with the storm and all, a lot of people left and never came back. And now you got all this FEMA money up for grabs, who knows what it's going to be like? Just saying that it used to be a rough place. There's boo coo lunch places but you wouldn't want to raise a family there. Do you own a gun?'

Todd gave it some thought.

'Nope. Never have owned a firearm. I used to shoot at squirrels and birds with my granddaddy's shotgun when we would visit the farm. Then Uncle Sam let me use an M16 for a couple of months. I mainly just toted it around a lot. I never used it except for target practice.'

'So I take it you were in the military. Did you get drafted?'

'No, I joined the reserve just after my eighteenth birthday. Even though we were pulling out of Vietnam, the draft was still foremost in everyone's mind especially my mother's. Nixon's going around saying he's going to end the draft but she didn't trust that. You can understand what with my dad being MIA in Korea, that plus Nixon being Nixon. She got me to join the reserve just in case. Then six months later, wouldn't you know it, Nixon actually ends the draft. Couple of months after that we are out of Viet Nam. Wouldn't have had to go anyway. I sure know some who did though.'

Todd paused for a moment. He thought of the older kids he knew in school who did have to go. Then he made a fist and knocked twice on the wood table. Ronnie got it. He continued.

‘Whoa, that’s been a while. Back on the gun thing, I’m just not sure. Or am I making too big of a deal out of your question?’

‘Maybe you are. I come from a long line of gun people especially on my mother’s side of the family. Back in the day they ate what they could shoot. Plus it helped keep everybody neighborly even if they weren’t the best of friends. But if you’re not a gun person you’re better off without one. Unless you’re willing to use it, a gun is a liability.’

‘Okay. I’ll keep your advice in, uh, advisement. By the way you’re right about my neighborhood. The LGD used to have its share of homeless. I got a grand tour of the whole neighborhood. This guy seemed to really know what he was talking about. Apparently he’s one of those old time New Orleans people you told me about. On some streets there were some wine and liquor bottles lying around. But there were lots of people walking around and nobody seemed all that freaked out by it. Overall the neighborhood seems okay. Supposedly the police are providing real good security nowadays. I understand the city has them picked up each day.’

‘Are we talking about bottles or people?’

Todd smiled.

‘Okay, I admit that part is a little bit of a bummer. I’ve lived in some pretty run down Memphis neighborhoods back in my day, so nothing I’m not used to. But what fired me up was the house. It’s what I think of as a classic old New Orleans house. Needs some work but they’re helping me out with that. It’s kind of a shotgun house only it’s a two story.’

‘That’s called an over and under shotgun Cher.’

‘Yeah well there’s a cool front porch and it’s got a lot of fancy wood work’

Now Ronnie seemed pleased. She found Todd’s enthusiasm infectious.

‘Don’t get me wrong. I’m happy for you Cher. I don’t mean to be trashing your neighborhood. I just want you to end up someplace nice. So tell me about this guy, this big shot you met with yesterday.’

‘Well, he is the actual project director, the head honcho. He took me to lunch to this place called Delacroix’s and then showed me around the neighborhood. I didn’t figure on that. Evidently he’s taking a lot of personal interest in the success of this project. Like you he’s very passionate about New Orleans. And he’s a good guy. Kind of a political rock star from what I gathered yesterday. We went into this private dining room in the back of Delacroix’s and everybody there knew him. He worked the room like a pro. His name’s Sal Leblanc.’

Ronnie’s eyes widened and she gasped.

Chapter 12 - Wiltz 'Huey' Fitzhugh

Sal had been obliged to move today's meeting with Todd back an hour to 11:00 am. Yesterday while showing Todd around the neighborhood his schedule had been pre-empted by a much more pressing meeting at 10:00 am, a command performance with the boss. Sal hoped to keep it short but he was prepared to cancel the meeting with Todd should the need arise.

Sal's boss was one Wiltz 'Huey' Fitzhugh. His official title was City FEMA Director. He was in charge of all the neighborhood directors citywide. His office was located downtown where Canal Street dead ends at the Mississippi river in the posh BP International Tower. Huey was a 'dyed-in-the-wool' local. He came from an old Irish family that had settled in the Irish Channel neighborhood nearly 200 years earlier. The nickname 'Huey' was a play on his surname as well as a nod to Louisiana political legend Huey P. Long. Like Sal, Huey had paid his dues over the years in various non elected public service positions. He was the classic middle manager type. His official job description consisted of dozens of pages of federal legalese. However the description of any middle manager job is basically as follows.

1. Never make a decision.
2. Always take credit.
3. First fix blame then fix the problem
4. When crap comes down from on high, keep it moving in a downward direction.

Items 1 through 3 could not be overemphasized. Huey had been taught by the best in the business. Regarding item 4, Huey's position in the FEMA chain of command was similar to that of a colonel in the military. He was well aware of the fact that the root word of colonel is colon.

Huey had known Sal for many years. They had worked together before. But this was the first time they had been in a direct reporting relationship. It was often necessary to put business ahead of friendship, a fact that was awkward to say the least. The early scams that had plagued the program had put Huey in the hot seat. Some of the local news had picked up on these scams and reported them, especially in the Florida panhandle. But the national media considered it to be small potatoes. They were interested in applying heat to the White House and the top FEMA brass. Good thing that. It would have been a political bloodbath. Huey likely would have had to sell his good friend Sal down the river to lessen the damage to himself. Things were still bad enough. In the French Quarter the number one selling tee shirt was one that said 'FEMA, the new F word'.

That was all history now. Sal's brainchild known as the Terpsichore Project had been favorable received. Today Huey wanted a status report on the project. The written reports all looked good. That was to be expected since they were produced by Sal's own staff rather than an independent agency. But like any manager worth his salt, Huey wanted the face to face skinny. That's the only way you could assess body language. Next week he would get his turn. He would be standing on the carpet in the regional FEMA director's office at One Exxon Square in Houston. When that happened, he wanted a good solid song and dance to give those cowboys.

At exactly 10:00 am Sal entered the City FEMA director's office. Huey's Office Executive Assistant was seated at the front desk.

'Hello Rosalie. How ya doin?'

'Hello Sal. Can't complain. You're early. Take a seat if you like. Oh, you know where the facilities are located, right?'

'Right, don't mind if I do. That's why I'm a little early. You know the Doc says I got a slightly enlarged...'

'Yes I remember your telling me that. I'll inform Mr. Fitzhugh that you're here.'

Rosalie wasn't being sarcastic about Sal being early for the 10 am meeting. It was a local custom to arrive a few minutes after the scheduled time. That was considered polite. To arrive too early was considered pushy. Some of the old timers actually took offense if you arrived too early. It was one of those New Orleans things that often tripped up out-of-towners.

When Sal returned to the reception area, Huey was standing there waiting. Not a good sign. He beckoned Sal to come into his office and suggested that Rosalie could bring them coffee. They made small talk until Rosalie brought in the coffee, then they got down to business.

'So Sal, financially your operation is looking good. Your expenditures are well documented and accounted for all nice and neat. Houston likes that which means I love it.'

'Yeah well, Debbie's got a good head for numbers.'

'I've said this before Sal. You really showed some initiative with this Terpsichore Project thing. To be frank, I thought you'd lost your mind, sticking your neck out like that. But in the end it saved our bacon. D.C. went for it in a big way. You deserve a helluva lot of credit for that.'

Huey paused for effect. Sal braced. Here comes the two minute manager routine.

'Having said that, all it's really done is buy us some time. Not to seem ungrateful, but what I need to know is do you have something to show for all these expenditures; some success story that we can build on. This is your baby Sal. But my big concern is Houston is saying 'what have you done for me lately'. They're getting a little impatient which means that I'm getting a lot impatient. Do I need to say more?'

Sal was tense but not surprised. He had been expecting exactly this kind of grilling.

'No, I hear you loud and clear. Let's not forget that this program is barely 6 weeks old. And we got all these consultants from out of town. They're like raw recruits and it takes a while to get them up to speed. But they're good at what they do. We'll get there. It just takes time. Tell Houston that.'

'I'll worry about what to tell Houston. So you're making good progress getting the consultants up to speed. What else have you done?'

'Okay, we've had a dozen or so inquiries over the internet and they're increasing. Most of them don't pan out. They lose interest once they learn they have to permanently relocate. But at least now we know ahead of time rather than finding out the hard way. And the bona fides applicants? They're out there. In time they'll come. Just yesterday we accepted our first one. And it's not like I'm just standing around watching. Hell no. I'm taking a personal interest in this Huey. I spent better than half a day with this guy. He's kind of a geek and of course he's an out-of-towner but he's gonna be the success story you talk about. He's interested and excited about making New Orleans his new home.'

There was a pause. Sal squirmed a little. Crap! Had he laid it on too thick? It was time for Huey to say something.

'That's better. How does he feel about the list?'

Sal tried to hide his relief. He was good at reading people, but Huey's poker face was impenetrable.

'He'll play ball with us. I explained the certification requirement. He understands that it's in everybody's best interest.'

Huey sat back in his chair.

'Good. That'll keep the locals happy.'

Sal was ready for the meeting to be over.

'We'll be finalizing the paperwork with him just as soon as you and I finish up here.'

Huey wasn't.

'Just the one guy?'

'We have a dozen or so prospects on hold. I'm taking it real slow. Don't want anymore scam artists coming out of the woodwork. Once we get that first success story things will start falling into place.'

Huey grinned a big toothy grin and leaned forward in his chair.

'And I wouldn't presume to tell you how to do your job. All's I'm saying is maybe you're being too cautious. You're way behind some of the other neighborhoods. Let's get the ball rolling with these other prospects. Maybe you could use some help showing the properties. I know this guy with Uptown realty. He's got realtors just salivating to get a piece of your Terpsichore gig. They could really get things moving for you. Why don't you give him a call? '
'I'm doing my best, boss. You and I both know my neighborhood

isn't exactly the favorite horse in the race.'

Huey was less than sympathetic.

'Sure I know that. Could've been worse you know. You could've been given one of the down river neighborhoods.'

Sal took a long sip of coffee while he mulled this latest comment/threat. He regained his composure and even managed to laugh it off.

'Yeah well. Hey, you know I'm a control freak. I admit I have issues with delegation. Okay maybe I'll call your friend at Uptown realty. Just cut me a little slack.'

'I'm afraid slack is in short supply these days old friend. Next week I'll be on the carpet in Houston. I need to be able to tell them that we have a dozen bona fide applicants to show for our expenditures. And I expect to do just that.'

'I won't let you down boss,' Sal replied.

Huey stood up. Suddenly he was all smiles and handshakes. The two minute manager routine was over.

'All right fine. You've told me what I need to know. I've got nine more of these scheduled today. And I know how busy you are. I'll walk you out.'

As they walked out, Sal checked his watch and turned to Rosalie.

'Good coffee Rosalie. Say would you call my office and tell Debbie we're on for our 11 o'clock meeting with Mr. Jamison.'

Huey offered his hand and they shook again, all palsy-walsy for Rosalie's benefit. Yeah right, as though she didn't know what had gone on in the meeting. Later that morning, she would receive the usual call from Debbie Cirlot to find out what find out what had taken place. And Rosalie would oblige her because, in good time, Debbie would have an opportunity to return the favor.

'Have a good day Sal. Let's have lunch when we're not so busy.'

'I'd like that Huey.'

As Sal drove back to Terpsichore HQ at 1450 Calliope, he mulled over his meeting with Huey. It wasn't what was said so much as what wasn't said. Houston was important but of greater concern were the local interests and their nonstop insistence on how best to dispense FEMA funds. All politics is local as they say and the locals had serious reservations about the Terpsichore project. It was in essence a bottom up process and for obvious reasons they preferred a more top down approach. Never mind the fact that there was more than enough money to go around. Everybody is always wants a bigger piece of the pie. But other than mentioning the list, Huey hadn't even brought up the locals. At least there's that to be thankful for. Or was it? There was a meeting in two days with the chamber of commerce who were pretty much synonymous with the locals. Was he being set up for an ambush at that meeting? He made a mental note to do his homework just in case. As he pulled into his parking space he had one more question. Was it too early for a hit of brandy?

Chapter 13 - Hair Like Elvis

Back at Teebow's, Todd had just mentioned that his meeting the day before was with a man named Sal Leblanc.

Ronnie gasped and exclaimed, 'Oh my God, Sal LeBlanc? I think I know him. I mean granted there's a lot of Sal LeBlanc's in the world.'

'Not in Memphis there aren't,' Todd added unhelpfully. Sometimes he just had to do that.

Ronnie was unperturbed. She was too elated.

'But if he's the same one, he was my boyfriend in junior high school. All the girls had a crush on him. He was so handsome. He had hair like Elvis Presley.'

'Yeah, not so much anymore.'

'He was real popular with the other boys too. He was a natural leader. He wasn't real popular with teachers as I recall. Always getting into trouble. Then he went on to high school. He was a year older than me. He met somebody else and we lost touch. All those years ago and I never quite got over him. Last I heard he was a limo driver for a lot of the local big shots.'

'Bingo. Now, that would be the one and the same Sal Leblanc. He told me that he was once a chauffeur and that it led to better things.'

'Do me a little favor? Sometime when you see him, just ask him if he remembers Ramona Chauvin. That's who he would know me as. But don't let on that it's any big deal or anything.'

Was Ronnie blushing? Was there still a lovelorn school girl

hiding inside her?

'I'll be sure to make it seem like it's no big deal. Wow, I need to duck in my room real quick. I'll bring the leftover food when I come back. Got a few Dixie beers left, too.'

'Definitely bring them. And don't forget to change shirts. The one you're wearing smells like fried oysters.'

Fifteen minutes later Todd returned with a leftover sandwich, four warm beers and a fresh shirt. Ronnie made a face.

'Sorry Cher, I'm going to have to say no more food in the room. Beer is okay, just no food. Here let me put that in a plastic bag. It might still be salvageable. Maybe I'll make some dirty rice or something.

'And while we're on the subject of housekeeping, could you dry off before you step out of the tub? Yesterday I practically had to put on my water wings.'

'Yessum. Sorry about that. I think I'll have me one more cup of your delicious coffee.'

'Yeah, yeah, yeah. So tell me some more about today. What all you got going?'

'I have two meetings. The first one is pretty cut and dried. Just some more forms to fill out. Shouldn't take more than an hour, but you never know. Then I have an interview with my prospective boss. That's the biggie. A lot depends on how that goes.'

'What kind of work they going to have you doing?'

'Don't know yet. Don't even know who I'm meeting with. I

reckon your junior high heartthrob will tell me in good time. All I know is that it's supposedly in my field of expertise. Ideally it'll be some computer type job where I don't have to sell anything or manage anything. I can just work my geeky magic for some project manager. If they like what I do, the project manager takes the credit. I get paid. Everybody's happy. If they don't like what I do, I get the blame, work a little overtime to get it right. I still get paid and everybody's still happy. You can reduce it down to a flow chart.'

'That's way over my head, Cher. But it sounds exciting, and important. So why no suit and tie today?'

'You know what? Yesterday I was driving back out here and the day had gone well and St. Charles was just awesome. The sun was shining through those big old trees and the light was reflecting off the cut glass on those big old houses. I felt like ripping that tie off. And I did. And it just felt right. The traffic was crazy and everybody's honking their horns. Next thing I know I'm joining the party, honking my horn like all the other motorists and they're honking back. I felt like I belonged. And today I decided the tie wasn't going back on.'

Ronnie approved.

'That's New Orleans for you Cher. Even rush hour traffic can turn into a party. This old town will flat seduce you if you're not careful. And you just showed me a spark of something I haven't seen in you before. I believe you going to kick some butt in that interview.'

'Yeah, right after I make one last trip to the room. I probably need to be hitting the trail anyway. Don't know how late I'll be getting back. Oh, and thanks Ronnie. Awesome breakfast. I almost feel like you've taken me to raise.'

‘Yeah well. Don’t forget to remember me to Sal Leblanc. We’ll leave the light on for you. Hey, write if you find work.’

When Todd left she began to cry. Later when she heard his car drive off, she got up and began her daily cleaning routine. With any luck she would finish in time to catch Hoda and Kathy Lee.

Chapter 14 - A Real Case of Puppy Love

Todd had a much easier time finding Terpsichore HQ today. Since being early was almost as dreaded as being late he drove around the block a couple of times then parked behind the building in the spot Sal had showed him the day before. Perfect. At 10:58 he was announcing his arrival to Debbie Cirlot. Todd was a little early and Debbie informed him that Sal was still in transit from a prior meeting with his boss.

'No matter, he'll be here shortly,' she said. 'You mainly just have to sign some additional forms to finalize everything regarding the property you've selected. I've got them all ready for you. I'll show you to the conference room.'

Todd wondered why it wasn't the same smaller room where he had filled out some preliminary forms the day before. He got his answer.

'Take a seat Todd. You can be looking over the papers but don't sign anything just yet. We'll need our attorney and a notary public present when you do that. Our attorney's office is in this building. I'll buzz him when Mr. Leblanc arrives. The official witness will be yours truly. But first you'll be interested in this advance check. It's for $1500. Just keep good documentation of your expenses.'

'Yeah right. Thanks. Do you know a good place where I can get this cashed?'

Debbie executed an Olympic 10 eye roll.
'Seriously?'

'Scratch that. Maybe I'll find me a bank this afternoon and open up an account.'

'You think, Cher? And seeing as how you're from out of town and all, if the bank gives you any grief about the check, just have them call me. Here's my card.'

Todd was unphased by the sarcasm. All he could think of was that she called him Cher.

Sal and the attorney walked in the conference room at 11:15 am Todd's initial take on the meeting turned out to be more or less accurate. It had all been cut and dry and in just under an hour all the documents had been explained, signed, witnessed and notarized. Debbie gathered all the paperwork and left to make copies for Todd's records. The originals would be kept on file in the office. The in-house attorney, having served his purpose, busily offered parting pleasantries and excused himself.

Sal explained, 'We're not done by a long shot. Why don't we finish up in my office?'

Following Sal's lead, they entered the office and without breaking stride headed straight for his private lavatory.

Todd took this opportunity to mention Ronnie Geracie. Sal didn't know her. Then he remembered that Sal would know her as Ramona Chauvin. When he mentioned Ramona, the look on Sal's face reminded him of the look on Ronnie's face when he had mentioned Sal to her.

'Wow! Yeah I remember her but I haven't thought about her in a while. We were childhood sweethearts in the ninth grade. When I moved up to high school, there was this new girl, a blonde. I let Ramona go. I haven't seen her since high school graduation. So how do you know her?'

‘She owns this little mom and pop motel where I’m staying, Teebow's Motor court. It’s out on Airline Highway.’

‘No fooling? Ain’t it a small world? So what do you think of her?’

‘Still trying to decide on that. I walked in there to stay just the night and before I knew it she had talked me into staying the whole week. She’s been a big help, though, getting me adjusted to New Orleans. She’s all but taken me to raise. In fact I told her as much. She even told me my fortune the first night I was there. That was a bit much. But I reckon she’s pretty lonely. She told me she’s been a widow for like 20 years. Am I rambling?’

‘A little bit.’

‘Okay long story short. When I mentioned you she made it sound like she had this huge crush on you.’

‘Yeah. We had a real case of puppy love. There’s no drink or drug that feels half that good. So what’s she look like?’

‘Good. I’m sure she would clean up quite nice.’

‘She still got the flaming red hair?’

‘Oh yeh. Well mostly I should say. I guess my final answer would be who knows? But she’s definitely got the red hair personality thing going. By the way she said that in the ninth grade you had hair like Elvis.’

‘Yeah well, not so much any more.’

‘Which is what I told her.’

Sal pretended not to hear.

‘I always wondered what it would have been like if we had stayed together. She was from good people, not well to do but good. Good New Orleans people. I didn’t understand that then. But I definitely get it now, now that I’m going through a pretty tough time on the home front. I’m talking a full course divorce with all the trimmings. I had to go and marry a effing trophy wife. From Natchez yet. Serves me right.’

Sal’s voice trailed off like he was talking to himself. He seemed lost in thought then snapped out of it.

‘Okay, we’ll table this for now. We have business to attend to. But I want to talk some more about this later.’

As they walked from the lavatory back to the office Todd asked, ‘So where do we go from here?’

‘Sit down and I’ll tell you. It makes sense. Your new job or I should say your prospective new job is with one of the consulting firms we’re using. Your new boss or I should say your prospective new boss is located in this building. They’re mostly PR types, good at presentations and selling their service. But I’ve convinced them that they’re in serious need of some computer expertise and they’re willing to pay for someone who fits the bill. They should be with what they’re billing me. Whether or not they go for you is up to you. They already interviewed one guy and he was turned down. Of course, should you not hit it off, we’re obligated under the terms of the program to find you something. But I can’t guarantee you it won’t be selling Lucky Dogs on Bourbon Street.’

‘Not that there’s anything wrong with that,’ Todd quipped.

Sal smiled. ‘Okay, smart guy. Alls I’m saying is this is your best prospect. I've set up a meeting for you. Your new boss will take you to lunch and explain the requirements of your assignment. She should be on her way as we speak. Her name is Brandi Mendelssohn.'

Chapter 15 - Brandi Mendelssohn

Brandi Mendelssohn's office was located on the top floor of the building. After Sal's office, hers was the most richly appointed. It had originally been two bedrooms. A wall had been knocked out to create a grand office space that encompassed two corners, two balconies and no less than eight windows. Most importantly, like Sal, she had a private bathroom. Her position was chief project manager for The Greatest Gentrification, one of the consulting firms FEMA had engaged. The name was an apparent play on the Tom Brokaw book titled, The Greatest Generation. The firm had a solid track record for gentrifying old inner city neighborhoods in its home base of Atlanta. Indeed Atlanta was a forerunner in gentrification. One could argue that Atlanta was where the very term 'gentrification' had originated.

Atlanta's phenomenal growth beginning in the seventies had been a real meal ticket for suburban developers. But at some point in the eighties, Atlanta's suburbanites began to grow weary of their 40 mile commutes. And it kept getting worse. Entire counties were being swallowed up by suburban sprawl. By the early nineties, living 'close in' became a practical alternative whose time had come. However, that in itself wasn't enough. Not in 'Hotlanta'. It remained for PR firms like The Greatest Gentrification to make urban living fashionable. And it had done so with great success. Enter the phenomenon of the young urban professional, or 'yuppie', yet another term to which Atlanta could arguably claim to have originated. It all came together at the right time and the right place. At the height of the yuppie movement entire warehouse districts had been razed and luxury condos had gone up in their place. This all translated to financial success for a plethora of consulting firms but The Greatest Gentrification was widely regarded as the best in the business.

While the firm's name might have seemed cheesy to some, to

Brandi it was a classic example of wordsmithing at its best. Cheesiness aside, a big part of making the inner city attractive to suburbanites was coming up with cutesy names for things. She had coined the name of the salad bar restaurant 'Lettuce Entertain You' as well as the omelet shop 'H. Dumpty'. The name and catchphrase, 'Terpsichore Project - A New Dance for New Orleans' had also been her idea. These feathers in her cap coupled with an immaculate sense of how to sell herself had earned her the title of chief project manager.

Brandi knew it was just a matter of time before she would be named one of the firm's partners. But being willing to relocate was an absolute prerequisite, even for a fast tracker like herself. The New Orleans project represented a huge career opportunity for her and she had jumped at the chance when it was offered to her. Nevertheless, she greeted it with quiet ambivalence. It was her first assignment outside the friendly, if somewhat sheltered confines of Atlanta. The Lower Garden District was a far cry from the yuppie enclaves of Virginia Highlands or Inman Park.

An even bigger adjustment had been the people. Brandi had always been a quick study in how to engage people but embracing the local color of the Big Easy was a real challenge. In particular Sal Leblanc presented a major obstacle to her usual way of doing business. At first she attributed it to his being 'old school'. But later she had to admit that he was smarter than the average client. He seemed immune to her usual persuasive tactics. Moreover he had managed to frustrate her efforts to go over his head. This strategy was the cardinal rule of consulting. It was key to establish contact and credibility with the client's superiors. Ideally the goal was to have the boss trust you more than his own people. This was surprisingly easy to do, normally. She had met with Huey Fitzhugh, Sal's boss, on several occasions but to no avail. Sal had Huey's ear and his deepest trust. She had been obliged to resign herself to a level playing field rather than one tilted in her favor.

Sal was a micromanager. He insisted on going over every recommendation with a fine tooth comb. He also insisted on input into every decision however small. In short he was a pain in Brandi's beautiful ass. But she had to admit that his ideas were good ones. And he didn't care who got the credit just as long as he got his way. More importantly, thanks to FEMA, he had deep pockets. Her billable hours were never questioned and the financials were exceeding expectations. Atlanta liked that. Bottom line, the relationship, while not what she or the firm was accustomed to, was progressing nicely.

Another thing she had learned about Sal was that whenever he told you about a problem, he would immediately tell you the solution he had in mind. His latest idea was a typical example. He complained that Brandi's consulting team was deficient in providing detailed reports. The usual reports were just not good enough for his bosses. Sal wanted customized, *ad hoc* reporting at a detailed level that would keep the FEMA chain of command happy all the way up to D.C. Brandi countered that it would require additional staffing which would in turn result in increased billable hours. Sal agreed and okayed the hiring of a dedicated software developer. After the initial applicant was turned down at Sal's insistence, he told her of a candidate he had in mind. There was this really sharp computer whiz from Memphis named Todd Jamison.

Brandi rolled her eyes every time she recalled this conversation. She had dealt with computer types before. Sharp was not a word she would use to describe any of them. And here she was, about to take the prospective new hire to lunch for an interview. Her power heels rapped sharply against the wood floor as she marched down the hall to Sal's office. When she reached the door she tossed her glorious jet mane, rolled her piercing dark eyes one last time and entered. Debbie sent her straight through to Sal.

Sal stood. Todd followed suit and turned to face his prospective new boss. Their eyes met. As Sal made introductions, Todd felt like he had turned into Gomer Pyle. Why couldn't he at least have worn a tie?

'Todd Jamison, this is Brandi Mendelssohn. Brandi is heading up our project. She even came up with the name Terpsichore Project. She's with the Atlanta firm, The Greatest Gentrification. They're looking to hire a software developer.'

'Mr. Jamison, how are you?'

Say something you dumb ass he thought.

'I'm, I'm good.'

Say something else, he thought, before she thinks you're a complete asshole.

'So is it just me or are all consultants from Atlanta?' he lamely offered.

'I have no response to that,' she replied coolly.

So far he was exactly what she had predicted. After an awkward pause she added.

'Sal tells me you're from Memphis, home of Elvis and barbecued ribs.'

It may or may not have been a slight but at her mention of Memphis, Todd felt something stir within.

'That we are. We play a little basketball there as well I might add.

Oh, and in addition to Elvis, we invented rock and roll, soul music, and the blues.'

Now would be a good time to stop. Predictably, he didn't.

'And you're from 'Hotlanta', that center of phenomenal growth. Or what Ross Perot might call that great sucking sound in the southeast. So how many corporate headquarters did Atlanta gobble up last month? Hewitt Associates? Russell Athletics? Holiday Inn?'

The game was on.

'Oh it's been so many I lose count. It's just not that big of a deal to us. It's what we consultants from 'Hotlanta' do. That is, when we're not cruising to the mall and the tanning salon in our Beemer's.'

Todd wasn't finished.

'You know people in Memphis are still hurt about Holiday Inn moving their corporate offices there. The whole idea of Holiday Inns originated in Memphis. Some things are sacred.'

'Not in 'Hotlanta'. We're even thinking about dismantling Graceland and moving it to Stone Mountain. It'll be the centerpiece of a new mega-mall there. We're going to call it the Elvis-O-Rama.'

'Well at least it's not going to Orlando to be a part of Disney World.'

'Hey, that's an even better idea.'
It was Todd's turn to have no response to that. Sal finally jumped in. He had been completely caught off guard. He needed to regain control. 'Hey, truce.'

Todd returned to normal reality and became contrite.

'Right. I should apologize. I'm just kinda nervous.'

Then managing a weak smile, he turned to face Brandi.

'Hey, we were just kidding around, right?'

At the same time Brandi silently gasped. How did she lose control so easily? It was completely out of character for her. Todd was not at all what she expected. He was pretty quick on his feet for a geeky old dude. And she had done pretty well in the exchange herself. She actually enjoyed the give and take. Todd had offered them an out. She took it.

'Sure, we were just having a little banter. I love Memphis. I go there all the time on business. Hey! Go Tigers Go!'

Todd responded in kind.

'And Atlanta, it's just amazing every time I have to, uh I mean get to go there,' he said gesturing the Braves tomahawk chop with his right hand.

'Truce then,' Sal asserted. 'So where were you thinking about for lunch?' And without waiting for an answer, 'I know just the place.'

Sal decided not to include himself. He'd already imposed on Brandi to set this up. Best to let them sort things out on their own over lunch. New Orleans food had magical powers. Sal's recommendation had been the Bluebird Grill. It was close enough to walk and so they did. It was one of those gourmet 'greasy spoons' for which the LGD was famous. There was quite a bit of lunch time pedestrian traffic to command their attention. This helped to minimize the periods of awkward silence.

As they approached the grill they noticed a few police cruisers parked outside. They weren't alarmed since Sal had explained that this was a sign that the food was good. The NOPD knew all the best restaurants in town. There was a short wait for a table. Todd took advantage of this opportunity to visit the facility. Per Sal's recommendation, they had requested a booth in the back dining room. This setting was much better suited to a business discussion. Todd was anxious to try the red beans and rice but was informed that this particular dish was available only on Mondays. He ordered the next closest thing which was black eyed peas and pig tails. Being raised on his grandfather's farm, Todd had no problem with pig parts. He rather enjoyed the look on Brandi's face when he ordered. Brandi ordered the crab salad.

'You know this is not the kind of place I would take a prospective hire in Atlanta,' Brandi offered. She was smiling.

'Well I've known Sal for all of 24 hours, but I'm guessing this is some 'locals only' place tourists don't know about. That's always cool to tell your friends back in Atlanta.'

Brandi raised her eyebrows and nodded in agreement. 'You know you're right, especially the senior partners. For some reason they love little hole in the wall places.'

The food arrived. It was simple but amazingly presented. Suddenly they were hungry. For the next few minutes they ate mostly in silence interrupted by the occasional comment of approval. The food was more than good it was platonic. In New Orleans eating was a form of communion. It was a bonding experience. By the time they had finished, all the rough edges had smoothed out. It was time to talk business.

'Okay Mr. Jamison.'

'Call me Todd please.'

'Okay Todd, here's what we always do,' Brandi explained. 'I'm going to let you tell me about yourself and why you want this job. We'll get into specific skills and requirements for this position later this afternoon in my office. So go ahead. Sell me on Todd Jamison.'

'I'm not a salesman. I couldn't even sell newspapers when I was a kid.'

'Bullshit. Everyone is a salesman. I'll help you. Just show me some of that same passion that you had earlier when you talked about Memphis. It caught me off guard but you totally had me with that.'

'Okay. I grew up in a small town but I've lived all my adult life in Memphis. I went to school there, Memphis State or University of Memphis I should say. Didn't have the slightest idea what I wanted to do other than find a good paying job and get out on my own. Lots of people I knew were majoring in ethereal people skill stuff like management or marketing.'

Todd saw Brandi shift her eyes askance and retreated.

'Sorry. Obviously there are people who are good at that sort of thing. Just wasn't for me. I wanted to learn how to do something. So I chose computer science.'

Brandi took a moment to consider what he had said.

'Okay. Now, a good way to tell people who you are is to tell them about your family. Would you care to share something more personal about your early life?'

'Sure. I'm an only child. Presumably that was by default not design. My Dad went to beaver right after I was born and never came back. He was on patrol along the 38th parallel, that's the border between North and South Korea, and was caught in the wrong place at the wrong time. The real irony of it was that the conflict had officially ended two years earlier. I can understand your look of surprise. Such incidents weren't common but they did happen and they were always kept quiet.

'My mother didn't remarry until later in life. But I'm from a pretty big extended family. I had plenty of uncles to teach me how to pee standing up. They were all concerned that I didn't become a mama's boy. Obviously I had a lot of aunts and cousins, too. They all helped to raise me. My mother got a job as a bank teller. She was good at it. Her boss always used to say she had a good head for figures. We got by. End of story.'

'Okay good. Now you can talk about your qualifications.'

'I'm told that you need the capability to do custom reports for whom I've gathered is a rather demanding client. Hiring a dedicated software developer will set you apart from your colleagues who rely on cookie cutter, one size fits all, vendor supplied software packages.'

Brandi interrupted, 'Okay, now you sound like you're reading from a script. Not that there's anything wrong with that. But you don't need to tell me that anyway. I already know that I need to hire someone. Sal made that quite clear. But why are you that person? That's what I need to know.'

'Okay. I'm an old man playing a young man's game. Let's just get that out of the way up front. But I'm good at what I do. Granted, since my days at State U, the technology has changed but I've stayed current. I'm a bona fide computer geek. Whatever you need I can do. And on the off chance that I can't, I can learn it.'

'Good. You've got me interested. I know what you have to offer. Now, to close the sale, kiss my ass. By that, I mean tell me why you want what I have to offer. It's always about the passion. I'm thinking I might want you. Show me how much you want this job. Show me just how much you want me.'

'Well first of all, my wife and I divorced. I didn't want a fight so I agreed to a pretty generous settlement with her. Then I lost my job shortly thereafter. Bad timing that. Long story short, I need the money.'

Brandi interrupted. 'Okay, there's a fine line there. You want to sound hungry but not desperate. Which I think you pretty much did. You gave it just the right touch of anger. Okay, go on.'

'It's more than the money, much more.'

Brandi raised her eyebrows in approval.

'I'm getting a second chance. For a dude my age that is one of God's great blessings. Do you know how many friends I have in Memphis who pound the streets looking for work? Who sit all day waiting for job interviews never to get called back? By the way, a lot of them used to work for Holiday Inn before it relocated to Atlanta. Ouch. I didn't really say that.'

'It's okay, just stay on message.'
'You want passion? Take a look around. The catastrophe of Katrina has made this incredible old town a frontier. Can you believe it? A 21st century frontier. Here for the taking. How special is that? It's a second chance for me and this town. We need each other. We're partners in this dance.'

'Shut up!' she exclaimed. 'I've just witnessed the birth of a salesman.'

She paused to put her professional face back on.

'Mr. Jamison, I mean Todd; I am prepared to offer you a position if you're still interested. As I said earlier, we'll need to go over some of the particulars in my office this afternoon. You can give me your response then if you like.'

'Actually, you had me way back at Go Tigers Go.'

The walk back to the Terpsichore building was more relaxed than the trek over. When they got back, Brandi had her office manager run down some documents while she and Todd waited in her office. She took this opportunity to discuss the requirements of this job. Todd listened and explained he would need a better computer than the laptop he brought with him. There might be some additional software packages he would have to purchase as well. Brandi nodded matter of factly and continued.

She had dealt with technical types before. The job required more than technical savvy. The client was a huge federal bureaucracy with many levels of management. This meant a lot of people throwing a lot of requirements at you all at once with a lot of last minute changes. Projects might pop up with little or no advance notice and would need to be completed asap. Asap literally meant asap. In situations where the project could not be accomplished in normal working hours, he would be expected to work extra hours with no paid overtime. All employees and consultants of the firm were paid a flat salary to get the job done whatever that might entail. No real problem, Todd had been there done that many times.

Now came the punch line. It would not be enough to merely do the work. He would also need to show professionalism.

‘It’s like this,’ she explained. ‘When the client wants something it has to be done with no objections. No ‘I’ve got a better idea’. No ‘it would make more sense to do it this way’. Just do it.’

Holy shit he thought. How much did she know about him? His old employer must have given Sal the entire personnel file which he no doubt had shared with Brandi.

‘Ouch. You’re rubbing salt into some old wounds, emphasis on the word ‘old’. You should check the dates on your information. Some of that was back when Reagan was in the white house. Back at the Bluebird you made it sound like a done deal.’

Brandi held firm.

‘I’m paid for one thing and one thing only, to keep the client happy. That can’t be over emphasized. This firm has a reputation for being among the best in the profession. And I’m working on a reputation of my own. It’s why I took this assignment in the first place. And if it all works out, I plan on being able to write my own ticket when I get back to Big A.

‘You’re right. This is a done deal. My firm wants to employ your services.’

Then a pause.

‘But if I’m asking too much then there’s such a thing as a deal breaker.’

‘Well it is refreshing that you’re telling it like it is. I like that. Most of my past issues, with which you seem to be so well acquainted, had more to do with people mincing words. And, inasmuch as you’re not given to that infuriating practice, I think we can do business.’

‘Okay Todd. There is one more issue. Atlanta is telling me no more employees. It’s just not in the budget. We are addressing all staffing needs with contractors. We’re looking for a contract programmer. Do I still have you?’

‘Actually, that’s even better. I’ve always wanted to be a contract programmer. We used them at my old job. They seemed to have it better than the employees. Didn’t have to go to any of the corporate indoctrination meetings. They weren’t pressured to participate in Political PAC’s or Savings Bond drives. So yes, you’ve still got me. The problem is I’m not familiar with Louisiana laws regarding self employed contractors. I’m sure there’s some licensing or certification procedure I’ll have to go through.’

‘We can get that done in a couple of days. We have an attorney in-house to handle all the legalities. But as of now you’re on the payroll so to speak. So welcome to the Greatest Gentrification team. We think we’re the best in the business. We hope you’ll come to agree.’

‘On the payroll is something I didn’t think I’d ever hear again. That reminds me I have some banking to do this afternoon.’

‘Oh that’s good. Your first day on the job and you’re asking for the afternoon off. I’m kidding. Actually I’m busy the rest of the afternoon. I need to call Atlanta and let them know you’re in. That’s liable to turn into a 3 hour conference call. Just be back here at 5 pm. We have some more papers to sign; some more business to discuss.’

Chapter 16 - Little Miss Can't Be Wrong

Todd was in luck. He was able to find a branch of his Memphis bank nearby. Since he didn't need to open a new account, this simplified getting his advance check deposited. With $1200 in the bank and $300 in his wallet he felt like a new man. He was also able to get the credit limit raised on his Visa. That would more than hold him until his first paycheck.

Upon returning to Terpsichore HQ he was informed by Brandi that Atlanta had empowered her to give him a grand and proper welcoming. The paperwork could wait until morning. For now she was more interested in taking him to dinner. Lunch had been nice, quaint; but she wanted to take him someplace befitting a new member to the team. It was all standard procedure in welcoming new hires. Hmmm, Todd thought, why am I feeling suspicious? Standard procedure for whom, the firm or for Brandi personally. No matter, either way he was agreeable. He was in the mood to celebrate. Now that he was able to relax, he found his new colleague attractive. She was quite striking. No doubt it helped her professionally. Then he realized he was getting caught up in a fanciful conceit. He remembered some advice from Uncle Bubba. Enjoy the curves but consider the angles. The angles, right. Okay granted I'm pretty rusty at this kind of thing. She's young, intelligent, assertive, goal oriented, used to getting what she wants. She's in familiar territory whereas I'm trailblazing here. But I have age and maturity on my side, right? I have wisdom going for me. He scoffed at this ridiculous internal dialogue. Fuck it. Don't over analyze. Just go with the flow and see what happens.

Initially, at least, that turned out to be a good tactic. Brandi had things all planned out. They exited the building and stepped right into the back seat of a waiting taxi. Todd thought what if he had refused the invitation? Obviously Brandi considered that possibility to be so remote as to be unworthy of consideration. The taxi took them to Canal Place.

Canal Place had long been a major tourist and convention site with its modern hotels, fancy restaurants and high end boutique shops. It was also convenient to the Louisiana Superdome. In the wake of Katrina, Canal Place and the Superdome had been among the earliest of FEMA beneficiaries. The idea being that as goes tourism so goes New Orleans. Accordingly they received huge capital infusions. These infusions had been sufficient to not only restore but greatly expand the convention district from Canal Place several blocks along the riverfront. This was the serious money. By comparison, the Terpsichore Project was small potatoes.

The drive from the LGD to downtown may as well have been to the opposite end of the galaxy. Gone was anything uniquely resembling New Orleans. They could have been at the convention district of any major city in the country. It was all glitz and neon. They were in a sea of tourists, conventioneers, gamblers and business travelers. In short, out-of-towners. They might as well have been in Atlanta.

'Isn't this just awesome?' Brandi exclaimed. 'It's almost like being in Atlanta.'

Todd looked into her face and forgot whatever he had been thinking. This highly professional woman had just become a four year old girl on Christmas morning. Over Todd's effete protest, Brandi paid the taxi driver. They walked past a uniformed doorman, entered the BP International Tower and rode the glass enclosed elevators to the restaurant at the top floor.

'So do you come here often?' Todd asked.

'Oh yes. I've had a few lunch meetings here with Huey Fitzhugh,

Sal's boss. His office is in this building. But I've never been here at night before. Okay, no more work. I'm ready to play. Let's hit the bar.'

The hostess led them to the bar which was located in the center of the restaurant. At Todd's suggestion they sat at the corner of the bar so that their faces were angled toward one another. Brandi liked that. The bartender came over to take their orders. Brandi wanted a dirty goose martini.

1. Grey Goose vodka,
2. straight up,
3. olives,
4. equal parts vermouth and olive juice.

Todd was impressed that she described it with such precision. Then remembering lunch with Sal at DelaCroix's, he ordered a sazerac.

'Going native are we?' the bartender said.

'Yeah well, I am a native, sort of.'

'Sounds like an interesting story. Wish I had time to listen to it. Be right back with your cocktails.'

'Well I've got time, in fact I've got all night,' Brandi said. 'Why don't you tell me your interesting story?'

'You've already heard most of it. I pretty much spilled my guts at lunch.'

The drinks arrived.

'So pick up where you left off. Your life didn't end with college did it?'

'Nice bait, but I'm not biting. It's your turn. You said you took this assignment as a career move. Sounds like you can't wait to get back to Atlanta.'

'Okay. I've got an idea. Instead of having you pump me for tidbits all night, why don't I just cut to the chase and tell you all my dirty little secrets. That's what you're dying to hear anyway. I'm a mind reader you know. It's an essential skill to being a good consultant.'

'No problem with having my mind read. Just the other night I had my fortune told.'

Then she took a big sip of her dirty goose martini and gathered her thoughts.

'Okay, my father is a surgeon at a big Atlanta hospital. He's done well. My mother technically is a *stay at home* but her volunteer work keeps her out of the house almost as much as Dad. She organizes charity fund raisers and serves on a lot of foundation boards. I grew up in a big house on Paces Ferry road. You've heard of mama's boys, well I'm a daddy's girl. I got a baseball glove for my 4th birthday. I never took any interest in baseball. Luckily for dad my brother came along right after that. But I kept the glove. It became a symbol. It taught me that limitations are for other people, not me. I was encouraged to go after anything I wanted and I did: academics, extracurriculars, boys… not necessarily in that order.'

She flashed a self conscious smile and took another sip. All for effect, she obviously liked talking about herself.

'And I was quite good at it, getting what I wanted that is. By the time I reached high school I had a reputation of being the ultimate Jewish American Princess.'

Todd raised his eyebrows.

Brandi rolled her eyes, 'Oh come on, spare me the feigned look of surprise. You've been thinking that ever since you first laid eyes on me.'

Todd tried to protest.

'No, that would never even occur to me.'

'Todd! Shush! I'm a mind reader, remember? Let me finish.'

She took another sip.

'It's not like it bothered me, not in the least even. People were just jealous. I was popular. I could have any boy I wanted and pretty much did. My folks weren't real strict on me. They spent a lot of weekends out-of-town, in the mountains or Hilton Head. So I'd have everybody over to the house for a big party. They trusted me to do the right thing and I did, for the most part. I made good grades. I never totaled the family car. I only got stoned at weekend parties and never at school. Like all my friends I got my own car my senior year in high school. Unlike a lot of my friends, I didn't get a boob job, didn't need it.'

Acting as though he hadn't noticed before, Todd gave a nod of agreement.

Brandi flashed another big smile.

'My dad used to keep his cigarettes and his Trojans in his top dresser drawer. My brother used to steal cigarettes. I'd steal the Trojans. Didn't usually need them but they came in handy more than once. I realize now how empowered I was compared to most kids. I grew up watching Ferris Bueller. He was my hero. High school in Atlanta in the 90's was totally crunk. It was Ferris

Bueller on acid.

'After high school Dad wanted me to go to med school but I wanted to be around sexier people than Medicare patients.'

'How's that working out for you?'

Brandi thought a moment then she got it.

'Come on, you're not that old.' She laughed and continued.

'Soooo, I decided to major in Business Marketing. I was accepted at the Fuqua business school at Duke but I just couldn't face leaving Big A for the likes of Durham. So I went to Emory and got my MBA there. After graduation, I scored a position with the best consulting firm in Atlanta which means it's the best anywhere.

'I got engaged but broke it off. Two weeks before the wedding yet. Mom got all verklempt and wanted to die. At first Dad wanted to kill me. He'd already spent a fortune on the wedding. But he was cool about it in the end. It was actually a heart to heart talk with him that made me decide to back out. I just wasn't sure.

'After that I went bohemian, at least for a Buckhead gal like me. I moved into town, first to Virginia Highlands and then Inman Park. And, thanks in no small part to 'The Greatest Gentrification', urban living became the acme of fashionability. It's the year 2000 and property values are going haywire. I moved 5 times in 5 years. One year I made more money flipping houses than the firm paid me.'

She paused.
'But never having lived outside Atlanta has come back to haunt me. This town may as well be another planet. Nothing I learned

in Atlanta seems to work here. Would you believe you're already my best friend?'

'Sounds like an overused pick up line. It's working by the way.'

After a self conscious pause, Brandi noticed their glasses were empty.

'I'm not really hungry. Want to get another round?'

'Hey, all I've done since I got here is eat.'

Todd got the bartender's attention and signaled another round.

'I'm feeling all talked out. Can it be that just like that I've told you my whole life story?'

'Well you barely touched on the travails of being the poor little rich girl. I'm sure there was a downside to all that on which you could have elaborated.'

Brandi faked a 'poor little me' smile.

'Oh, and you totally omitted the 'little miss can't be wrong' phase of your life which I dare say continues as we speak.'

With that Brandi laughed aloud throwing back her gorgeous thick mane. Someone else might have felt slighted. But she felt supremely entertained.

'I would drink to that if I had one.'

The bartender presently obliged.
She lifted her glass. 'Bravo or touché' or whatever. To all the little miss can't be wrongs of the world. But such liberties you take. The behavior profile on you says you suck at reading

people. How did you know it wouldn't piss me off?'

'Maybe I like to live dangerously.'

'Yeah maybe. I think it's more a case of 'fuck 'em if they can't take a joke.'

'You really are a mind reader.'

'I know people. I've also studied the aforementioned profile at some length.'

She paused, 'So it's your turn now.'

Todd tried to backpedal, 'You fuckin' turned down Duke?'

'I get that a lot. And nice try, but don't change the subject. You're on.'

'So where did I leave off at lunch?'

'Your uncles taught you how to pee standing up.'

'Right, speaking of, I need to find the little boy's. Excuse me won't you.'

'I'm not going anywhere.'

Brandi would learn in time that Todd's potentially greatest moments were often pre-empted by an untimely bladder issue.

While Todd tended to business, he took this opportunity to do some self serving mental arithmetic. She's practically 30 and I'm just barely 50. Plus she's not actually the boss. I'm a consultant and she's the client. She herself said that the first priority of a consultant is to keep the client happy. And she's one of the best in the business. He rather liked that juicy rationalization. It was one of his better ones. Then sensing that Brandi might have been a little miffed by the interruption, he returned post haste. He was right. Brandi was growing impatient.

'Sorry for the wait.'

'Okay, no more cop outs. Tell me from where all this glorious, tragic, self destructive anger comes.'

'Whoa, you flatter me. You make me sound complicated and interesting.'

'Maybe you are.'

Todd's reluctance was an act. He enjoyed talking about himself.

'You know you left me a tough act to follow. I can't imagine two lives being more different than ours. I didn't grow up watching Ferris Bueller. With me it was Beaver Cleaver. You may remember from watching the reruns. You talk about how empowered you were. So how empowered was the 'Beave'? I mean every time he comes up with an idea or takes any initiative, it backfires in his face. It's always like a total end-of-the-world disaster. He tries to go to Wally for help. But all Wally ever does is tell him that this time he's really up shit creek, and when Dad finds out he's gonna kill him. And Wally must be the world's worst snitch because the next day at school, everybody knows all about Beaver's latest dumb shit screw up. Beaver tries to keep it a secret but Ward, the father, inevitably finds out. Then there's this humiliating, often tearful confession. And in the end Ward, June, Wally and all of Beaver's friends agree that he is a cute, complete dumb ass. That's more the story of my life. So that's why everything I say or do has an undercurrent of fuck 'em if they can't take a joke. Just once I wish Beaver would have said as much to Eddie Haskell. And on top of all that, my real name is Theodore.'

He feared he might have been getting a little intense but Brandi seemed interested in his every word. It was obvious that she missed Atlanta. Maybe she meant what she said. Maybe he was her best friend, at least here in the Big Easy. Maybe he was the only game in town. All this emboldened him plus the booze was kicking in big time.

'So you're still with me so far?'

She gave an agreeable nod.

With equal parts of bravery and bravado he forged ahead.

'I liked it while ago when you cut to the chase about all the dirty little secrets of your life. Imitation is the sincerest flattery, so I'm likewise going to cut to the chase. You seem like a cut to the chase kind of person.'

'Yes I am. So start cutting already.'

'Okay so like you, I take a dramatic sip of my drink for effect, a brief pause and then I begin.

'Let's assume, for argument sake, and I know this is the farthest thing from your mind right now. And it is the farthest thing from my mind as well. So, are you with me so far?'

Brandi looked perplexed.

'Of course. Whatever the fuck you're talking about would never occur to either of us, I'm sure. I thought you were cutting to the chase.'

'Okay. Let's just assume that we were trying to hook up. Who could be more exactly wrong than us? It's like the movie 'The Graduate' only in reverse. I'm Mr. Robinson and you would be like Benjamin Braddock's sister.'

'Shut up,' she exclaimed. 'That's the most totally crunk thing I ever heard.'

'Oh! I'm sorry. I knew I shouldn't have brought that up.'

'No! I'm right with you! Keep going!'

'One of these days I'm going to learn what 'shut up' and 'crunk' mean. Which, by the way, just beautifully proves the point I'm trying to make.'

'Whoopty shit. So you're an older man. Do you realize what cocky, immature jerks most men my age are? Besides, and don't take this wrong, the pickings here are pretty slim. I'm surrounded by local bureaucrats and political appointees who are, to a man, family men. And in case you haven't noticed, people here are wary of out-of-towners. Besides the Mrs. Robinson Graduate thing worked out pretty good in my opinion. It was the daughter that screwed everything up.'

Todd continued the argument that he hoped to lose.

'Okay. Be that as it may, what about the mixing business and pleasure aspect of it? Consider how complicated it will be back in the office.'

'Complicated for whom? Certainly not for me. It's no big deal. Not back in Atlanta anyway. You couldn't possibly be expected to know this but in a workplace where no one is over 35 that kind of mindset is considered, well, a quaint old fashioned notion. And that's the real issue, differences in mindset, not age.'

'Yeah I guess maybe. You're right about one thing, a workplace where no one is over 35? That is something rather foreign to me. Now a workplace where no one is under 35, that's a scenario I can easily envision.'

Time for more drinks. By the end of their third round of cocktails, Todd's argument was not so much resolved as forgotten. They decided to forgo a formal dinner and eat at the bar instead. This approach is a great way to sample a restaurant's menu, especially in New Orleans. The bar menu consisted mainly of appetizer dishes. They each ordered one of every oyster dish of which there were no less than five.

As the food began to arrive, the conversation became less back and forth and more a waltz of words. Their differences became points of interest rather than obstacles. Somehow it became easier to focus and easier to hear each other. It was no longer necessary to shout to be heard. The faces and the din in the background seemed to fade away. They were alone in the crowd save for the periodic revisiting from the bartender.
After gorging themselves on oysters and finishing a fourth round of drinks Brandi's perfectly clipped 'valley girl' diction had taken on the slightest bit of slur. Todd's trace of rural twang had become full blown Tommy Lee Jones.

She placed her hand on his, leaned over and spoke into his ear, 'Hey Beave, I have a proposal.'

'Okay.'

'If you be my bodyguard, I can be your long lost pal.'

Todd waved at the bartender. He offered to pay. He was more

sure of himself now and this time Brandi let him with the condition that he would be later reimbursed. The bartender looked approvingly at the gratuity. He deserved it and knew it. He had made the drinks progressively stronger. Todd's last sazerac had been almost half absinthe. As they walked away he called out, 'Thank you sir, enjoy our fair city.'

Brandi started to say 'My place or yours'. But before she could finish, Todd said 'Yours'.

'Good I can show you my baseball glove'.

They took a cab back to Terpsichore HQ and got in their respective cars. Todd followed Brandi almost bumper to bumper in an effort not to lose her. When a traffic light turned yellow at just the wrong time he nearly rear ended her. That would have been Freudian in the extreme he thought. Brandi was living in a rental house just over in the Garden District. Nice digs as Todd would have expected. She gave him a cursory tour of the house which ended in the bedroom.

Brandi's passion was overwhelming. Like all high achievers she knew what she wanted and how to get it. And Todd? He allowed himself to be overwhelmed. In all his years of professional and social mishaps, he had at least learned one thing. When something good happens to you, let it. He was just glad to be there.

How long it might last was anybody's guess. Brandi had made it clear that for her New Orleans was a temporary blip in her career that would move her toward some greater long term career goal. It was only a matter of time that she would complete her assignment and return to Atlanta. Todd had made it clear that for him New Orleans was a new dance, a new life. It was his best and only prospect. And so with eyes wide shut, he resolved to make the most of the moments they shared together.

In retrospect this time would seem like a wonderful and magical stretch of the road. Viewed from a real time, day to day perspective, there would be some significant bumps in that road.

Chapter 17 - Should I Stay or Should I Go

The decision of whether or not to stay the night took care of itself. Todd passed out. The next morning he compulsively awoke at his usual 6:58. It took a couple of seconds to remember where he was and a couple of minutes to realize that he had a serious hangover. As appealing as Brandi looked, and felt, lying against him, his base instinct told him to get the hell out of Dodge. Like Cinderella's carriage at the stroke of midnight, she had turned back into the boss. Luckily Brandi was not a morning person. In under 5 minutes, he was able to get up, dress, pee and leave without disturbing her. No time to leave a note, nor any need. She would figure it out easily enough. Such was his thinking in the moment.

He remembered Brandi's house was a block and a half off St Charles Ave. From there he could find the way back to Teebow's. As his hangover fully began to kick in, Todd tried to figure out his next move. Damn he could sure use a mug of Ronnie's coffee. Fifteen minutes later he was getting his wish. He was also explaining the previous evening, as best he could, to an interested and suspicious Ronnie.

'So it turns out my boss is a woman. Who knew? Technically she's not my boss, we're associates. I'm an independent consultant. I don't actually work for her.'

'But she tells you what to do? She signs your paycheck, no?'

'Yeah well, that's true.'

'Forgive me if I don't see the difference.'

Why was he feeling so defensive? Being taken to raise had its drawbacks. But he'd always known that. He took another sip of coffee.

'I told you I'd be out late, last thing before I left here yesterday.'

'Not no all night long you didn't tell me.'

'I had a lot to drink. The bartender must have doubled up on the last couple of rounds. I knew you wouldn't want me driving back in that condition.'

'And so you spend the night in her house? Did the boss tell you to do that?'

'Sort of. Well no, I'd say that it was mutual.'

Ronnie could roll her eyes as effectively as could Brandi. 'Sort of? So this woman, this boss of yours, you gonna bring her around for me to take a look? I can tell you if she's any good for you. It's part of my fortune telling gift.'

Todd had expected this kind of reaction. It didn't mean he was prepared for it. He decided to go with shameless flattery.

'Of course I'll bring her around. She's led kind of a sheltered life. She's never lived anywhere but Atlanta. Even here she's mostly surrounded by people from Atlanta. I want her to see real New Orleans people. I want her to taste some real New Orleans home cooking. And I want you to explain to her all those important things you explained to me.'

Ronnie saw through the ploy but softened a little despite herself.

'Yeah, that's all I'm talking about Cher. The bark is worse than the bite. You know that by now, right? Just don't mince words. Don't ever bullshit a bullshitter.'

Ouch that hurt. But the coffee was kicking in. His hangover might have lessened a little. Suddenly he remembered.

'Hey I mentioned you to Sal Leblanc yesterday. He remembered you.'

'Really! What did he say?'

'A pretty good bit. Actually the look on his face may have said even more. He wanted to know how I knew you and I told him I was staying the week at your place. Then he talked about how you were childhood sweethearts in the ninth grade. He said you were from good New Orleans people. He wanted to know if you still had the flaming red hair and I told him yes.'

Ronnie flushed slightly and looked away.

'Yeah well, with a little help.'

'He also mentioned that he's in the process of getting a divorce.'

By now the previous evening was but a distant memory.

'Did he say anything else?'

'Not really. We didn't have a lot of time. But he seemed really interested. Said that he wanted to talk some more later. I'll probably see him sometime today.'

'Well let me get your breakfast going. We don't want you to be late. Just give me about half an hour. Why don't you go clean up in the meantime? You smell like oysters.'

'Well I should. I ate about two dozen last night.'

Ronnie got up and headed to the kitchen muttering.

‘That is SO not what I’m talking about.’

Todd poured himself another mug of coffee and went back to his room to prepare for the day. He was patting himself on the back for defusing the situation. It would prove to be a good warm up. The day was young.

Chapter 18 - A Three Mile Kind of Day

Brandi woke up at 10:15. It took her a minute to recall the night's events. Where was Todd? Did he just split? Probably just as well. Maybe he left a note. That would be nice. Nothing. Dammit, he could have left a note. Then she noticed the time. Enough rehashing. Live now.

First order of business was to call the office and inform Brad she would be coming in after lunch. Then she would ask him to arrange a meeting with Todd Jamison at 2:00 pm Now that she had bought herself some time, she set about to nurse her hangover. She brewed a single cup of French roast and grabbed a small container of yogurt.

When she got the coffee and yogurt down it was time for her customary morning run. As dreadful as it seemed, she knew from experience it would help. It was later than she usually ran but the longer she waited the more intolerable the heat and humidity would be. She picked out an appropriately conservative running outfit. A quick last minute bathroom visit and then out the door she went.

As usual she headed uptown on Prytania. St Charles was popular with most runners but she found it too noisy and crowded. She had a six mile route which consisted of running to Audubon Park and back. But by the time she got as far as Lafayette cemetery she realized it was going to be a three mile kind of day. The edge that usually drove her to go the whole distance was missing today. She decided to turn around and walk back through the cemetery as she caught her breath. Being an Anne Rice fan she fancifully checked the corner crypts for sleeping vampires. As the initial exertion subsided she began to feel better. Once out of the cemetery, she paused in front of Commander's Palace restaurant to check out the menu that was always posted on the front. She ran back on Coliseum and managed to make it all the way to the house without stopping.

Back at her place she downed a bottle of water and brewed a second cup of coffee. She took her coffee upstairs and sat out on the balcony for the express purpose of sweating profusely and breathing in the thick steamy air. Back in Atlanta her friends were paying $100 an hour at some spa to sweat out a hangover. Free steam and sauna was a perk of living in New Orleans. As her head cleared a little she began to relish the revelry of the previous night. Since moving to New Orleans it had been too much work and not enough play. The trips back to Atlanta were fun but they were too few and far between. She missed evenings like the one last night and looked forward to more. She tried to remember. At one point did he tell her she was getting a good deal on a used car? She laughed aloud. This old boomer was a hoot and a half. If mom and dad only knew. It was going to be a good ride. Something to do anyway. Can't let him off too easy about skipping out though. That will come up last thing in their 2:00 pm meeting at the precise moment when he thinks he's gotten off the hook. How must his head be feeling about now? Worse she hoped. Despite her hangover, she finished her coffee with a smile.

Todd was en route to 1450 Calliope when he had a major 'Oh Shit!' epiphany. He realized he should have touched base with Brandi before running out. He couldn't remember when and where he was supposed to report today. He didn't even know if it had been discussed. What the hell was he thinking earlier this morning. His head began to spin and his hangover started to get worse. Okay what's the plan? He'll just have to fake it. He'll walk into Brandi's office like all is well and see what happens. Something would surely come to him. If not he could just play dumb and nerd his way out of it which wouldn't require a lot of acting skill. Not the best plan but a plan nevertheless. At least he wore his suit and a tie today. At 9:58 he entered Brandi's office. He recognized the office manager from the day before.

'Hello, I'm Todd Jamison. We met briefly yesterday. I believe it's Brad Casey isn't it.'

'Yes. What can I do for you?'

Todd assumed his most businesslike body language.

'It was my understanding that I had a meeting with Ms. Mendelssohn. Am I not on the schedule?'

Brad spent entirely too much time fumbling through some notes while Todd nervously waited.

'Brandi won't be in until afternoon. Your meeting with her is scheduled for 2 pm There must have been some miscommunication. However there are some forms we will need to fill out and get you to sign. I suppose we could get you started on that in the meantime.'

Todd breathed a sigh of relief. Brandi was still at her place.

'I'll also need to get licensed as a self employed consultant. I met with an attorney yesterday over some real estate matters. I believe he can help me with the licensing procedure as well.'

'Ah. Glad you mentioned that. There is a note attached here. That's actually the first order of business for you today. Our attorney's name is Guy Martin. His office is just down the hall. You're supposed to be there now. When your business with him is done just come back and I'll have all the paperwork ready for your contract with us. Tell you what. Guy doesn't have an office manager right now. That's a bit awkward. Why don't I show you in. Just good office protocol.'

Guy Martin was African-American and with the exception of 4 years in the military he had lived his entire life in New Orleans. He had been able to further his education with the help of the G.I. Bill. He had done his undergraduate work at Xavier University and gotten his law degree at Loyola. He struggled with the minutiae of academics but managed to make decent grades.

As a clerk he proved to have good legal instincts. He might not always be able to cite the exact case but he was good at remembering all the landmark court decisions and the reasoning behind them. He had envisioned becoming a trial lawyer or defense attorney. But without belonging to an established firm it proved a hard business to break into.

After Katrina all the law firms had stopped hiring anyway. Being a public defender was always an option but there wasn't a lot of money in it. He had grown up in the Ninth Ward with a couple of friends who were now in city hall and knew Sal. They helped him land his current position. The FEMA gig paid the bills and working for Sal was a piece of cake, for the most part. But he found it boring, routine and legalistic. Arguing a case before a judge and jury was the real action. He looked forward to the day when he would be able to establish his own practice.

Guy's office was smaller than Brandi's office but just as handsomely appointed. Brad entered the office, introduced Todd, confirmed that he was expected and left.

'So Mr. Jamison, you can call me Guy. May I call you Todd?'

'Please. We barely said hello yesterday. You were in and out in such a hurry. They must be keeping you pretty busy.'

'Yeah, it's a knack.' He paused to be sure Brad was gone. 'Appearing to be busy that is.'

'Let me just verify. You need to get licensed to practice as a self employed consultant in the state of Louisiana. Right?'

Todd nodded.

'Okay, the license application has to go through Baton Rouge and that will take 4 - 6 weeks. There is no provision in the state of Louisiana for a temporary license but there is a way around that. You don't need a license until you've earned more than $50,000. I'm guessing that won't happen before the license is approved.'

'You're batting a thousand.'

'And since you're now self employed you won't be having payroll tax withheld from your paycheck. We'll need to get you set up to file estimated taxes on a quarterly basis.'

'Okay if you say so. But I need to set up an LLC or a P.C. or a special K or some kind of hocus pocus corporation. And I need a taxpayer ID. You can help me with that right?'

Guy was in his element.

'Sure I can. That's what most people want to do. They've been led to believe that setting up a professional corporation results in lower taxes and protection from being sued. People in my profession profit from that misconception. Going that route would net me an additional 10 to 20 billable hours.'

'Okay, so why am I thinking you're going to tell me different?'

'I believe in the KISS philosophy as in keep it simple. I've been told that the best software developers subscribe to that philosophy as well.'

'Yeah I like to think that's what I do.'

'Well as your attorney, if you'll pardon the expression, I recommend setting up a sole proprietorship. That way you just use your social security number as a taxpayer ID. That will save you between 10 and 20 billable hours from me. It also greatly simplifies filing your taxes. That will save you another 20 to 30 billable hours each year from some tax accountant. And forget about limited liability corporations. There's no such thing. The only limit to liability is how much money you have. Anybody can sue anybody. That's the one given in the legal profession. The only insurance against being sued is, well, insurance. Now I don't imagine that software developers get sued that much, but I have read about a case where a program error resulted in the software company being sued. And the programmer who wrote the code was sued personally, not to mention fired. Which brings me back to my original statement.'

'Anybody can sue anybody,' they repeated in unison.

Todd just remembered something.

'You know something like that actually happened to me once. I used to write code for a payroll system. I once had to work 48 hours straight through to fix a software problem so that the company wouldn't get sued. The fact that only I could fix the problem was all that kept me from being fired. Then there was another time when a typographical error in my source code almost caused a union strike because overtime was being calculated incorrectly.'

'Sounds like I'm preaching to the choir.'

'Sounds like I've hired me a good attorney. I'll go with all your recommendations. How much insurance do I need?'

'You need to talk to an insurance agent for that. I just happen to know someone.'

'That's good.'

'And of course it goes without saying that you need to keep your personal and business finances completely segregated. That means separate bank accounts, credit cards, etc.'

'Of course. Looks like I'll be making another trip to the bank this afternoon.'

'You'll need to hire the services of an accountant as well. I can recommend a couple if you like.'

'I'll do that too. Thanks.'

'Good. But first things first. Let's get this license application going. As you can see I don't have an office manager so Sal is offering the services of Debbie Cirlot. She's just amazing. Based on what I was privy to yesterday she should have all the necessary information on file already. I'll get her started on the paperwork right after we're done here. All we need is your John Henry on the dotted line and tomorrow the application will be on its way.

'Now that still leaves the matter of your contract to provide services to The Greatest Gentrification. TGG will need to draw that up. It's pretty cut and dried stuff so that will probably be done by tomorrow if not later today. Of course I get paid to look it over to make sure it's legal and proper. Again, you sign on the dotted line and that's it.'

'Yeah I already talked to Brad about the consultant contract. I need to be doing that now assuming we're done here.' Todd turned to leave. Guy stopped him.

'You busy later on? I'd like to take my newest client to lunch.'

'I'd like that but I am kind of busy this afternoon. Big meeting with Brandi. Plus per your counsel I have some more banking arrangements to take care of. How about tomorrow?'

'Tomorrow it is. Just drop by the office anytime after 11:00 am. I'm wide open.'

'So far I've had somebody take me to lunch every day. Getting kind of spoiled. Today I'll get to see how I do fending for myself.'

'Lunch is a way of life here. You can't go wrong in this neighborhood. Hey do me a favor and don't tell anybody about my schedule being wide open tomorrow. I have an image to maintain.'

'Your secret's safe with me, Guy. You did say you're buying right?'

It took a little over an hour for Brad to draw up the particulars of his contract. Todd initiated a lengthy discussion over whether he would legally be contracting with TGG or with Sal directly. Ronnie's earlier comment about Brandi signing his paycheck was still burning his ears. He would have much preferred working for Sal rather than Brandi. But argue as he might that was quite simply out of the question. Todd's contract represented additional billable hours that TGG would pass on to FEMA, i.e. Sal. They were not about to give up their piece of the Todd pie.

By noon Todd was done for the morning. Being on his own at lunch was a change. He decided to try out his sense of direction and find his residence at 1256 Terpsichore. He hadn't learned the order of the streets and it him took a while. He ended up getting a good tour of the neighborhood in the process. When he spotted it a sense of deep satisfaction overtook him. It looked even better than he remembered. The years of neglect had only given it more character. He couldn't believe that this would eventually be his home; that in the weeks to come he would see it transformed into something special. This one of a kind old jewel of New Orleans was his. What stories the walls could tell if only they could talk. He struggled to take it all in. It was too good to be true. He felt grateful beyond words. Yet it was all tinged with a sense of survivor's guilt. He thought of the misfortune of others that had afforded him this opportunity. His path had led him here. And it made sense that someday his path would lead him to a time and place of reckoning, a place perhaps where he would be obliged to pay it forward. And when that happened, he would face up to it. After all it was only fitting. It was the natural order of things. In the end, the debits always equal the credits.

Enough of the existential shit, time to find something to eat. From his previous trips, he had learned that when in doubt there is always beer and oysters. So he ducked into the first oyster house he encountered. Evidently he had made a good choice because everyone looked local. He studied the scene and decided the cool thing was to stand at the bar where you could eat oysters mere seconds after they were shucked. Behind the bar he could see huge burlap bags filled with fresh caught oysters still in their shells. It must take two men to handle them. He ordered a Jax beer and a dozen oysters. After observing the other patrons for tips on how best to eat an oyster, he ended up drinking them from the shell so as to get all the tasty juice. It reminded him of the time years ago when he had watched a farm hand drink a can of pork and beans for lunch. The bartender talked as he shucked. He informed Todd that a true native could walk in, down a beer and a dozen oysters and be back at their desk within the 15 minutes allotted for their afternoon coffee break. Todd learned something else. Although he ordered a dozen, he ended up eating more like 15. Another advantage to standing at the bar. Evidently the bartender didn't count so well. Despite Todd's compulsion for numerical accuracy, he didn't point out the discrepancy and left a nice gratuity. As he walked out he felt as though the universe and the bartender were smiling. It was paradise and lunch. What made him think of that? He'd heard that somewhere before?

He still had plenty of time to go by his bank. There, per Guy's recommendations, he set up a separate bank account for all business related deposits and expenditures and applied for a business credit card.

Chapter 20 - The Conference Call from Hell

After his lunchtime activities, Todd had some time to kill before his meeting with Brandi so he hung out with Guy for a while. It was becoming awkward not to have his own office. He was grateful that Guy didn't seem to mind. In fact he rather seemed to enjoy the opportunity to bend Todd's ear about the pros and cons of being on retainer versus direct hourly billing. Some time later Debbie brought by the completed license application. Guy looked it over and showed Todd where to sign. That afternoon it would be in the mail on its way. Guy was right. Debbie was good at what she did.

Brandi had wanted to meet in her office at 2:00 pm. At 1:58 he thanked Guy and walked down the hall to Brandi's office. He wasn't sure what they would talk about but it didn't matter. He found himself looking forward to being together. It seemed like days rather than hours since he had seen her. Just the thought excited him.

When he saw Brandi again he felt a warm fuzzy flush wash over him. It was going to be difficult to stay focused on business.

Brandi apparently had no such problem. Rather, her problem seemed to be strictly physical. 'Hello Todd, have a seat. How's your head?' she asked rubbing her temples.

'My head's not too bad. I had some strong coffee for breakfast and a couple of antidotes at lunch.'

'Hmmm. We need to compare notes on that sometime. How was your morning?'

'It was actually very productive. I got to know Guy Martin a little better. We've applied for a state contractor's license. It will take six weeks to get that approved but he assures me that in the meantime I'm good to do business for TGG.'

'Good, then. We'll need a copy of the application for our files of course. Brad may have mentioned it, we're still working on your contract. It should be ready for your signature tomorrow. You'll be paid the going rate.'

'Great. Before I can sign it Guy says he'll need to look it over. Just a routine part of his job. I'm sure it will be fine. I'm just glad to be working. A more immediate concern is ....'

'Your office. I was just about to address that. We're pretty maxed out in this building. There is space available a few blocks away in our field office. We were going to locate you there with some of our property research and restoration specialists. But Sal made it clear in that way of his that he wants you in close quarters. So he's in the process of making room for you here.'

Hmmm. That's a good thing Todd thought.

'Okay so when?'

'You'll have to see Sal about that. Maybe when we're done here. Which brings me to the real reason I called this meeting. Yesterday I called Atlanta to confirm your contract. You're our first contractor on this project and one of our senior partners wants to have a conference call chat with you.'

She looked at her watch. 'Brad will be hooking us up in about 5 minutes.'

Todd began to squirm. He cleared his throat. 'Thanks for all the advance notice.'

‘Brad forgot to tell you? Don’t hit the panic button. Your contract is a done deal. This is just a welcome aboard kind of thing. You should be flattered.’

‘Senior partner heh? What’s he, about forty?’

‘Almost. I should warn you he’s sensitive about his age.’

‘I totally suck at this type of thing. Do I have time to run down the hall real quick.’

Brandi smiled knowingly. ‘I’m way ahead of you big guy. You can use mine. It’s through the door on the left.’

As Todd left, she added, ‘Be sure to leave the seat down.’

When Todd returned, Brandi handed him a note pad.

‘Here, I’ve written down some talking points for you. You can practically read this verbatim. Just remember how you were yesterday at lunch. You’ll be fine.’

Todd still seemed distracted. Suddenly Brandi got up and walked over to him. Before he could react, she sat down on his lap, gave him a brief twerk and returned to her seat.

‘That was an attention getter. Now focus on what you have to gain not on what you have to lose. If it makes you feel any better, I have my own cliff notes too. And you can bet that Atlanta will have theirs as well.’

‘Theirs? How many people are going to be in on this conference call?’

‘Just saying. If it’s a slow day some of the others may be interested in feeling you out, and me as well. You know I’ve got more skin in this game than you do. I'm the one who recommended engaging your services. So don't go all Beaver Cleaver on me.'

'Right. I'll try to hold onto that thought.'

Brandi's desk phone beeped. She pushed a button. Brad's voice came over the speakerphone.

'I have Sanford Andson, Kincaid Grady and Tara Cahill on the line. I've got them on hold.'

'Are we muted?'

'Of course.'

'Okay good. Give us just a moment. Write those names down. Here I'll do it.'

She wrote down the three partners' names and handed Todd the note.

'No Mr. or Ms. okay? First names are fine. Sanford is the senior partner. Tara and Kincaid are associate partners. They're expecting you to be a completely clueless geek. Maybe you can surprise them.'

Todd turned his attention to the talking points.

'Okay Brad you can unmute us now.'

Another beep signified the hook up was completed.

'Hello Sanford? Can you hear us?'

'Yes. Is that you Brandi?'

Conference call etiquette was tedious at best. After all the introductions were made, someone on the Atlanta end asked a question.

'So Todd, Brandi tells us you're a software engineer.'

'Yes that's correct.'

'Did you by any chance attend The Institute?'

Todd was puzzled. Before he could say anything untoward Brandi mouthed the words Georgia Tech. And again for emphasis, Georgia Tech.

Todd got it.

'Er actually no. You're referring of course to Georgia Tech. It is a great school. I attended the University of Memphis,' he said with as much pomp and circumstance as he could muster.

After an underwhelming silence, Todd felt obliged to go on.

'You may remember Memphis and Georgia Tech were in the same basketball conference some years back.' And under his breath he mumbled, 'We used to beat you with some regularity.'

Brandi heard him and made a face of disapproval.

After another brief pause a female voice asked. 'So tell us a little bit about your family? Are you married?'

'Uh, recently divorced.'

'Any little ones? Children that is?'

Brandi looked incredulous. 'I told them that already,' she

whispered.
Todd was just before losing it. Brandi had seen that look on his face the day before. He replied by quoting a line Uncle Bubba had often uttered. 'No. None to speak of.'

There was silence on the other end then some scattered nervous laughter. Todd buried his face in his hands.

Kincaid claimed to have been beeped and excused himself. Brandi knew that trick all too well. She also knew it was a bad sign. She made a disapproving face at Todd and pointed to the notepad. Stick to the script, she mouthed. It was time for her to jump in. After redirecting the flow of conversation she set Todd up for his monologue. Todd paraphrased as best he could from the talking points Brandi had prepared for him.

'Look I know how busy everyone is. We're all really slammed here and Brandi tells me that it's just a madhouse in Atlanta.'

Even though it was obviously a slow day in Atlanta, Todd could hear grunts and other sounds of agreement on the other end.

'So I think I can say we're all on the same page there, right?'

There were more grunts and harrumphs.

'Well, that being the case why don't we just cut to the chase. I'm just going to lay all the cards on the table. As I told Brandi yesterday, I am an old man playing a young man's game. The technical world has changed drastically but I'm confident that I've stayed current in my skills. And yes I'm fairly unattached especially for someone my age. Otherwise I probably would never have left Memphis. But by the same token I'm not looking back. I'm firmly focused on the future. This is a new start for me as well as the city. I'm committed to this opportunity I've been given. I believe in what TGG is trying to accomplish here. And more than that, I've talked to some of the local neighborhood people and they all agree that your firm is bringing an incredible positive energy to this town. Something it so desperately needs. It's exciting and I'm just glad to be a part of it.'

Brandi nodded approvingly.

Sanford replied, 'Yeah well, we try. That's very good to hear, especially from the locals. And your attitude is most encouraging. We're all proud of Brandi even though I fear she sometimes feels we've thrown her to the wolves.'

Todd decided to ad lib.

'If you say so Sanford. I would never have guessed that from being around Brandi. She is nothing if not the consummate professional.'

With that, Brandi's expression clearly said he was overdoing it. To emphasize she made a throat cutting motion with her index finger. Then she laughed off Todd's effusive comment.

'Okay, let's just get back to our newest member of the team. Any other questions for Todd?'

Sanford replied, 'I think we've taken up enough of your time. I'm comfortable with our decision and I think I speak for Tara and the other partners as well. Welcome aboard, Todd. And now I've got to run. Another meeting across town. I'm so glad we had this little chat.'

Todd referred to the talking points. 'It's mutual I'm sure. Thank you for your time.'

Brandi spoke. 'Tara I assume we'll have our daily status call at 4 pm as usual?'

'Yes, I'll double check with Kincaid to be sure.'

'Just let me know. Okay we're signing off here.'

When Brandi was sure they were disconnected she let out a deep breath.

'Well that happened.'

Todd agreed. He felt drained, as though he'd been holding his breath the whole time.

'I tried to tell you it was a bad idea.'

'Don't think I didn't try to talk them out of it.'

'It's not like I've had any experience dealing with corporate executives. But in all honesty, they weren't what I expected. Some of their comments were just, not very good.'

'When you're a partner, you don't have to be good. People revise reality for you to make sure you look good. But for what it's worth, I think it went pretty well. Tomorrow when it's had time to get around I'll see what's on the grapevine.'

'And for what it's worth, I think you're awesome. The little lap dance was brilliant. It worked.' Todd began to get up. 'Can I assume we're done here?'

'Keep your seat Beave. Let's talk about this morning.'

Brandi ended the meeting with some personal business. She politely read him the riot act. He had left her that morning, still sleeping, without so much as a note. How was that supposed to make her feel. After much listening and much contrition, Todd tried to explain. He apologized for being so inconsiderate. He had experienced panic, something akin to an out of body experience. He agreed that he had acted impulsively. He also promised that should there be any future liaisons, and he was by no means making that assumption, she would always awaken to a fresh brewed cup of French roast coffee at her bedside. By the time a truce was reached it was close to 4 pm It was just time enough for Brandi to prepare talking points for the daily status call with Atlanta.

As for Todd, it had been a long day. He had been obliged to defuse two stressful situations plus absorb and process a lot of legal advice. Then there was the conference call from hell. It had been a lot of unchartered territory to explore. He decided to have a quiet dinner back at Teebow's. Maybe a little chit chat with Ronnie would be just what the doctor ordered. He would wait until morning to inquire about the status of his new office. It was a good decision. Little did he know that tomorrow would have even more uncharted territory in store for him.

Chapter 21 - Sam's Pool Hall

At 10:00 the next morning Todd dropped by Sal's office. Debbie informed him that Sal was holed up in his office preparing a speech he was to give at a luncheon with the Chamber of Commerce. He frequently attended these functions. They were very important high profile affairs. His boss 'Huey' Fitzhugh was going to be there as well. Debbie further explained that Sal had made it clear that he was not to be interrupted for any reason. Granted they had just met. Nevertheless this sequestration struck Todd as very un-Sal like.

Debbie spoke on Sal's behalf. She assured Todd that everybody knows how awkward it is not having an office. Sal wanted him to have a good office here in HQ. But space is tight, so it's taking just a little while. They were working frantically on it. People were even coming in over the weekend. Sal will be back in the afternoon. He can see you at 3 pm if you like.

Thus assured, it was back to the street. He had some banking to do. By the time he'd finished with his banking business, it was a little after 11:00 am. He remembered his lunch date with Guy. Come by anytime after 11:00 am he had said. Taking Guy at his word, Todd dropped in and found him reading a law book with his feet propped up on his desk.

'You ready?' Todd asked.

'I've been ready,' Guy answered. 'How's your pool shooting because this place where we're going is a also a pool hall. They just so happen to have the best po boy in the city.'

'I'm a little rusty, but back at State U, I practically majored in Eight ball. Beat the hell out of studying.'

'I heard that,' he said, slamming the law book shut. 'Let me lock everything up and we're good to go.'

'You know I was under the impression that I already had the best po boy. I went to a place called Segway's in Metairie.'

'Yeah I've heard all about Segway's. Evidently a lot of people think it's the best but then a lot of people don't know about where we're going. In fact a lot of people wouldn't go where we're going.'

Todd wasn't sure he liked the way Guy had phrased that last comment.

'Are we walking?'

'No this place is down river a ways.'

They got into Guy's car and headed toward what was, for Todd, unfamiliar territory. He began to feel a sense of foreboding. They headed north to Claiborne which took them east for several blocks bypassing the French Quarter. Then they drove down river through the neighborhoods of Bywater, Ninth Ward, and Arabi.

Guy was taking them through the part of town that had suffered some of the worst of the flooding. Rather than offer any commentary, he chose to remain silent. By the time they reached their destination Todd was visibly shaken. They were at a place called Sam's Pool Hall. He wasn't sure if he was in the mood to eat.

'You okay?' Guy asked.

'Yeah, I'm not feeling very hungry just now.'
'Maybe I should have warned you but that's my old 'hood' we just drove through back there. It's been about a year since Katrina and

it might as well have been last week. I wanted you to see it first hand.'

'Yeah not that big of a deal really. Sometimes stuff just gets to me a little bit.'

'So why don't we talk about it over a cold beer and a game of eight ball and take it from there.'

'Sounds like a plan, counselor.'

Chapter 22 - Damage Control

After her usual early morning ritual, Brandi arrived at the office at 10:00 am. She looked over the latest status reports from the property appraisal specialists. They were charged with the meticulous task of researching and evaluating, one by one, every property in their assigned area. They did research all the way back to the original construction where possible. Then they documented all restoration issues and came up with recommendations on how to bring these properties back to their original condition. It was real bean counting stuff, a virtual sea of minutiae through which to navigate. And they were doing an incredible job. Evidently some people enjoyed that sort of task oriented work. At least at the end of the day they're off the clock and free to do whatever. They could just leave it all behind at the office. More power to them.

Brandi however didn't have that luxury. As project director, it remained for her to ensure that these recommendations were well received by the all important Lower Garden neighborhood committee, the historical society, and of course Sal Leblanc. Then there were the partners back in Atlanta who needed to be kept constantly informed. It was necessary to be always reading people and assessing their reactions. This balancing act demanded a certain political acumen. It often kept her awake at nights but she was equal to the task. It paid much better as well.

Speaking of politics, it was time to check in with Atlanta and assess how Todd's introductory conference call had been received. Brandi learned early on to always give lip service to the official chain of command. But in actual practice, the chain of command has limitations. If you want to know what's really going on, you go to the grapevine. And the unimpeachable sources for tapping into the grapevine were the 'powers behind the throne'. They were the unofficial eyes and ears of the organization. Accordingly, she had cultivated close relationships with the office managers and executive assistants by showing them the same respect that she would to a partner or associate. She made a point of never forgetting a birthday, of never being too busy to notice the latest family photo on the desk, and of always showing appreciation and gratitude. This stood in contrast to the 'taken for granted' treatment they usually received from their bosses.

Using her cell phone instead of the office phone, she called Macie Keller. Macie had been Brandi's office manager prior to her transfer to New Orleans. She was older than Brandi and lived 'way out west', in Douglassville. Initially she had shown reluctance toward Brandi's ethnicity. But that proved to be short lived. Brandi treated her with respect, something to which she was not accustomed in her early life. Plus Macie had a heart of pure gold and soon became the very picture of loyalty. She was good at what she did and had been an invaluable aid to Brandi in her career advancement. Macie had expressed true sadness when she learned of Brandi's transfer. Brandi of course had shown the courtesy of privately telling her before it was officially announced. Brandi made a habit of talking to Macie at least once a week and not just when she needed something. For Macie's part, she relished these weekly chats. They always made her feel important. She was genuinely happy to help Brandi in any way she could. She missed Brandi and looked forward to the day when she would return to Atlanta and be promoted to partner. A promotion for Brandi would no doubt be a promotion for her as well.

After a few minutes of personal chit chat, Brandi asked about the previous day's conference call. Macie's reports were always brief and to the point. After many 'under the breath' telephone conversations with her contemporaries, she had gotten feedback from virtually all the key sources. Sanford Andson, the senior partner, had been the most impressed. That was key. Kincaid Grady had become impatient and bailed early so his less than flattering take was discounted. Tara Cahill had tried to ruffle Todd's feathers and more or less succeeded. But it had been more a dig at Brandi and was seen for what it was. Some of the other partners had comments as well. Evidently they had eavesdropped on the conference call. A clear violation of telephone etiquette but being partner had its privileges. The consensus was that Todd had done about like they expected, maybe even better.

Macie saved the best for last. She knew that Brandi was interested in knowing every little detail about Tara. In closing Macie mentioned that Tara was overheard to say 'Sounds like he's right for the job. But thank God we didn't let Brandi hire him as an employee. What was she thinking? I mean a geek from Memphis State?'

Brandi expressed her thanks and they hung up. All was well. After enjoying a brief moment of satisfaction her thoughts turned to Tara and her all but predictable dig. Tara was an arch rival but an important role model as well. She had been the firm's first female partner. Brandi had learned a lot from her.

'That bitch!' she said aloud.

Chapter 23 - The Broke Dick Dog District

A million miles away at Sam's Pool Hall in Arabi, the game was eight ball. Todd had won the toss and made the break while Guy fetched a couple of beers. The beer was in cans and was so cold it almost hurt his throat. He could even feel its coldness whenever a swallow hit his empty stomach. Todd sank a few shots then missed. Guy then proceeded to run the table. Todd's game was good but he was no match for Guy. After losing three straight games, Todd held up his hands in mock surrender.

'I give.'

'I thought you said you majored in pool.'

'I did. I didn't say I was any good. Maybe I could eat something after all as long as it's not another helping of humble pie.'

'Why don't we split a 'Fats Domino'. It's a roast beef po boy big enough for two. In fact to eat a whole one, you have to be Fats Domino. That's how it got its name. New Orleans comfort food at its finest.'

There were no tables so they sat on stools at the counter amidst gallon jars of pickled eggs and the largest dill pickles Todd had ever seen. The Tabasco sauce was in containers the size of ketchup bottles.

Guy introduced Todd to Sam Dubois, the proprietor. They finished their beers while Sam retreated to the kitchen to make the sandwich. It arrived all smothered and dripping with gravy on a woefully inadequate paper plate. Thankfully it also came with a generous stack of paper napkins. At Sam's insistence they had two more beers. After one messy bite Todd's nerves felt better already. The cold beer was helping as well. As they ate their sandwich Todd used the lion's share of the napkins.

Guy explained, 'You know, a real veteran here at Sam's can eat one of these and play a game of pool without getting so much as a single greasy fingerprint on the cue stick.'

Then he turned to Sam.

'Todd here is the new kid in town. I'm showing him the ropes. The drive over still has him kind of shook up.'

Todd and Guy were preoccupied with eating. Except for them, the place was empty so Sam grabbed a cold beer pulled up a stool and proceeded to hold court with his captive audience. What followed might well have been dubbed the 'soliloquy from hell'.

'So you're the new kid in town, huh. Welcome to the 'Broke Dick Dog' district of New Orleans. Now granted you won't see that in any tourist brochure but it's what the people who live here or rather who used to live here call it. Are you familiar with the term broke dick dog?'

'Well no. But after driving down here, I get the general idea. A picture is worth a thousand words.'

Sam barely waited for Todd to finish his comment.

'Yeah well, be that as it may, I'm gonna give you the thousand word version anyway. The BDD got its name way before Katrina. You ever hear of Hurricane Betsy?'

Todd shook his head no.

'That's okay, most people haven't. And them that do have forgotten about it. It hit this neighborhood back in 1965. I was 12 years old at the time. Now Betsy wasn't nearly as bad as Katrina but it was bad enough. It should have been a wake up call to anybody with a room temperature IQ. But that was forty years ago and people, especially politicians, have short memories. A lot of people don't realize it but everything down river from the French Quarter to the Ninth Ward is a peninsula. Water on three sides. Then you get to the Lower Ninth ward which is virtually an island. Surrounded by water and below sea level. To the south we got the river. To the north we got the lake, And on the east and west we got man made canals. Man made! And that's where most of the flood broke through, the canals. Citywide the canal walls were breached in over twenty places. On top of that the pumps fail because they're not designed to work under water. I know. Go figure. You might could say the flood was a man made disaster just waiting to happen. You might could even say we were lucky it took as long as it did for a Katrina to hit.'

Sam paused for effect.

'Yeah, lucky all right! Lucky as a broke dick dog. Now some independent group from out in California came here and did a study. They concluded that those twenty levee breaches were the worst engineering catastrophe in U.S. history. Wow! Give those dudes the Nobel prize.'

Todd's social skills weren't the best but he knew better than to comment. He just shook his head in sympathy trying to fathom Sam's frustration. Sam looked Todd in the face for a moment. Evidently he found Todd's response acceptable. He continued.

'Now as Katrina approaches, our good mayor strongly recommends we lock up our properties and evacuate, which I did. Luckily I live alone and I got family in Baton Rouge where I can stay for a few weeks or months as it turned out. Six months later when they let us come back to the neighborhood, I find the front door of my house was knocked in leaving the house wide open to looters and vagrants. I later find out why. The National Guard was going house to house looking for bodies. When they couldn't get in, they fire axed their way through the door. I would have been better off just leaving the door unlocked. After the looters took everything, squatters moved in and trashed the place. So much for the so called curfew. It did a good job of keeping out the rightful owners, but squatters and looters, not so much.

'Then I find out real quick-like that the squatters aren't going to leave without a fuss. I'm severely outnumbered. My mama didn't raise no dummy, so rather than take things into my own hands, I go to the police. They send me to the small claims court. Now I always thought the term 'squatter's rights' was sarcasm or an oxymoron. Wrong! It turns out squatters do have rights. The judge says I have to go through due process. Translation, I have to hire a lawyer and prove I own the property. Luckily I happen to know a pretty good one.'

He nodded toward Guy and continued.

'Long story short the judge finally issues an eviction order. The next week the police show up and 'relocate' the squatters into some leftover FEMA trailers.

'So I'm back in my own house surveying the damage trying to get some FEMA money so I can get things in order. At least the electricity has been restored. Then a week later I get a delinquency notice from the power company saying I haven't paid my bill in 6 months. Two days later they shut my power off.'

Todd had no response but responded anyway.

'That's just unbelievable. You know what I mean. I'm not actually saying I don't believe you.'

Guy, who had heard it all before, continued to eat. Sam killed what was left of his beer and burped impressively.

'I'm not through yet. How about another beer?'

Todd and Guy declined.

'Fine. Suit yourself. I'm having one.'

Sam returned and continued.

'So as not to come across as a pessimist, there is some good news. It took forever for me to talk to an actual human being at the power company but once I do I tell them what I just told you. And they see things my way. Two weeks later I receive a bill marked paid in full and I have power again. Imagine that. Also on a good note, my house is just a block from the river levee so I only have three feet of flood damage. The floors are salvageable. The walls are all good. There's just some foundation damage. I guess that's why the vagrants chose my property. I suppose I should be flattered. It's not like I'm complaining. I'm a 'glass half full' kind of guy.'

Guy shook his head. It was gallows humor at its best. Sam remembered he was supposed to be making a point.

'And that is why we call this neighborhood the Broke Dick Dog district. Because we wouldn't wish it on a broke dick dog.'

Sam softened.

'You know what? The really sad part of this story is I am one of the lucky ones.'

Sam gave out a little half crazed laugh.

'I can't wait until tomorrow because it just keeps getting better every day. But like I say, I can't complain. So that's my story. I just have to tell it every so often, get it off my chest. Thanks for listening. The cold beers and the food are on me.'

'Thank you but Guy was buying anyway.'

Once again Sam burped impressively, as if to voice his sense of irony.

'Did he tell you that? He knows his money is no good in here.'

Guy jumped in.

'That's how he pays his legal fees, with cold beer and po boys.'

'Don't forget the free pool,' Sam added.

Just then a young attractive African-American woman entered the front door dressed in a food server's uniform. Sam noticed the time and got up.

'Hello Camilla. Right on time as usual. Todd this is my niece, Camilla.'

Then Sam excused himself.

'Time to get cracking in the kitchen, gents. The afternoon tour bus will be here in 45 minutes. We're real popular with the tourists. We make the best po boys in town. Plus as you can see for yourself, there's no competition this side of Bywater.'

They shot another game of eight ball. This time Todd won. He suspected that Guy was tanking.

In parting, Sam shook Todd's hand.

‘It’s been a pleasure. You’re not as Opie as you look. That would be Opie as in Sheriff Andy’s boy you understand. Glad to have you down here in the BDD. Now that you know where we are don’t be a stranger. Come by anytime. And don’t listen to what uptown folks might say about us. You’ll always find the same respect that you bring with you. I personally guarantee that.’

Sam’s comment reminded Todd of Ronnie’s advice to respect everything and everybody. As they drove back upriver he was curious.

‘Did Sam say something about a tour bus?’

‘Yeah, the Lower Ninth has become a real popular tourist attraction. Other neighborhoods were badly damaged but all the focus was on the Lower Ninth. We can thank the national media for that. There’s still a barge resting on top of a collapsed rooftop. The city left it there because they said it’s our version of a 9-11 type ground zero memorial. Plus it’s the highlight of the Ninth Ward tour. Sam has real mixed emotions about it. It offends his pride but it’s good for business.’

‘So does he still live here, in the Ninth Ward I mean.’

‘Yeah, we were able to get him a homestead settlement from FEMA to restore his house. This was early on after the storm. Back then they were just handing out cash with little or no procedure. So he didn’t have to live in a trailer. He didn’t lose any family. Like he said, he was one of the lucky ones.

‘Now before Katrina, Sam’s business establishment was located in the Ninth Ward as well. The reason he moved to Arabi is because getting a commercial settlement out of FEMA is a much more complicated than getting a homestead. Because of all the national focus on the Lower Ninth, homesteads were getting priority over business grants. So I advised him to relocate his business to a suitable property in Arabi, which is just over in St Bernard parish. That worked out a lot better. Just a simple matter of the lines being shorter in St. Bernard parish which is not as populated, and not nearly as political. Does that make any sense to you?'

'Sure. It's just that I hadn't even noticed that we were in a different parish.'

'Yeah well, Bywater, Ninth Ward, Arabi. It all looks pretty much the same. Something else I bet you don't know is before the storm the Ninth Ward was over 90% black, Arabi was over 90% white. But Katrina she don't care about that. It's all the same to a storm. A hurricane is the ultimate equal opportunity employer.'

'You're right. I didn't know that. Something else I don't know. Why did you bring me here?'

'Would you believe because I like you?'

'It's an interesting way of showing it. Don't get me wrong, it was a real hoot meeting Sam. I can't believe his attitude. He actually has a sense of humor about all this.'

Guy thought for a moment.

'You seem like an upfront kind of guy. I'll be upfront with you. In a way, I hijacked you. You never would have come here on your own. And here you are, an out-of-town white boy, getting a fresh start, all fat dumb and happy, so to speak. I don't know. I just wanted you to feel my pain. I wanted you to hear Sam's story, not the spiel they give you on the tour bus. No offense?'

Guy offered his hand, Todd accepted.

'No offense. Even if there were, I probably deserve it anyway.'

Guy gave Todd a puzzled look.

'Just a little knee jerk guilt,' Todd explained. 'It's a white thing. You wouldn't understand.'

Guy still looked puzzled but then laughed and shook his head.

'Okay. If you say so.'

After that they rode in silence for a while. As Todd took it all in for a second time, its impact seemed even greater. He had let his defenses down. As powerful as Sam's words had been, that wasn't what was getting to him. It was the weight of unspoken words, the loss of home, the loss of loved ones. It was the radioactive residue of all the human anguish and suffering that had taken place here. It seemed to be coming up out of the streets, the sidewalks, the collapsed houses and the empty lots. He was reminded of a line from some old sixties song about 'ghosts crowding the fragile eggshell mind'. He had felt a touch of this the other day when viewing properties on Terpsichore Street. But it was nothing like this. Then a realization came over him. He didn't dare look Guy in the face. But he had to ask.

'So how about you Guy? Did you lose any family?'

There was a pause.

'Yeah Mammy, uh my grandmother. I was across town. The streets were all closed off. I couldn't get to her and she refused to leave with any of the evacuation teams. She didn't make it.'

'Todd felt like his heart would break in two. An awkward sob dry heaved through his chest.
'Are you okay?' Guy asked.

Todd just nodded. It was a while before he could speak.

'I'm sorry for your loss. You know, we all called my grandmother Mammy. She loved being called that.'

Guy nodded and said, 'Is that right?'

Chapter 24 - The Seans and the Brads

Guy realized he may have made a mistake taking Todd downriver cold, with no advance warning. He had wanted Todd to see the full extent of the devastation, the Ninth Ward in particular which was his old neighborhood. But he didn't expect that Todd would have such a strong reaction. In an attempt to be conciliatory, Guy made small talk the rest of the way back. It seemed to help. Todd was able to participate in the chit chat without having to think too much.

By the time they arrived back at Terpsichore HQ, Todd realized that his honeymoon with the Big Easy was over. He felt as though he'd been living in a fool's paradise. But his lunch tour with Guy had happened for a reason. It was an intended and necessary stretch of his path. It was better to be wiser even if you were somewhat sadder in the process.

It was two hours before Todd had his 3 p.m. meeting with Sal. Guy invited Todd to hang out in his office until then. Todd politely refused. He had done that the day before and it had been awkward. He felt like he was imposing on Guy's hospitality. Plus his legs felt restless. Since arriving in New Orleans, he had fallen behind on his jogging. His normal running week was a minimum of 20 miles and so far this week he had done exactly zero. His legs felt like he could walk all the way to the Teebow's Motor Court and back. But most importantly, in his current state of mind, he couldn't bear the thought of being cooped up indoors for two hours. He had to get out. He decided to go with his legs. He made the short walk down Calliope to St Charles Avenue and from there he followed the trolley tracks uptown. The heat and humidity didn't bother him. He welcomed this release and soon got into a rhythm. When just under one hour had expired he turned around and backtracked. He had become quite sweaty and decided to take the trolley. Riding in the open air trolley proved to be only a slight improvement.

At 2:58 pm he entered Sal's office. Debbie sent him straight through to Sal. Sal noticed that Todd had worked up a pretty good sweat but didn't comment.

'Come on in Todd. Shall we do our customary trek before we get started?'

'Love to,' Todd replied.

As they entered Sal's private men's room Todd tried to make conversation.

'You know this is quite a facility. It reminds me of the one at the Top of the Peabody. Ever hear of the Peabody Hotel? It's in Memphis.'

'Yeah I've been there. It's nice.'

Sal wasn't in the mood for chit chat and cut to the chase.

'Look I ran into Guy Martin out in the hall a little while ago. We need to talk. We done here?'

Back in the office, Sal continued.

'Let me say this about Guy. He's had an extremely hard time since Katrina. I took a chance giving him this job. Fortunately for the both of us, it paid off and he's gotten his feet back on the ground. But obviously he's still struggling with it.'

'Yeah I know.'

'He uh, he told me all about taking you to lunch. Said y'all went downriver. I'm not sure what was up with that. But he did tell me he was a little concerned with your reaction. He said he offered to let you wait in his office but you refused. Are things okay between you two? More importantly are things okay with you personally?'

'Yeah. I mean it's true that I was a little shaken for a while. I wasn't sure why he wanted to take me there. But he explained some things. He had his reasons. Bottom line, he bought me lunch. He even let me win a game of eight ball. It's all good.'

'So I don't need to revisit this with Guy?' Sal still wasn't convinced.

'Whatever problem I might have, it's certainly not with Guy. I'm sorry if he got that impression. As far as turning down his offer to chill in his office, I just didn't want to impose, not two days in a row. Besides I needed to take a walk. Get some air.'

'For two hours? It took you two hours to get some air? In this heat? Come on Todd don't bullshit a bullshitter.'

'Look, sometimes stuff just gets to me. Okay, maybe it did, or does make me feel a little guilty. Like you said the other day, I'm lucky. I feel like I need to be doing something. Something to help others who aren't so lucky, instead of just helping myself. I feel like I'm taking when I should be giving. You know?'

'Yeah, I do know. And you just validated my concern. You're not about to go all 'Hollywood feel good' on me are you?'

Todd was puzzled by this last remark. Sal was looking him dead in the eye. He had seen that look before. Like from his high school basketball coach when the team had just blown a 10 point lead.

‘Do what?’

‘Never mind. You want to help? Here’s what you can do. You can finish what you’ve started here. Look, I’ve seen the devastation up close and personal. I know exactly what you’re talking about. You don’t have the market cornered on survivor's guilt. I’ve lived in New Orleans my whole life. I know every neighborhood and the people who live there. So I feel like I can speak for the entire city. We all appreciate your sympathy. But we don’t need sympathy. Sympathy is highly overrated. And we don’t need no feel good missionaries from Hollywood. What we need is citizens, common ordinary productive citizens who will work here and live here and get this town functional again.’

Sal studied Todd for a moment.

‘You look as blank as a sheet of paper. Am I making any sense to you at all?’

‘Yeah. It’s just you’re laying some heavy stuff on me. I’m trying to take it all in.’

‘Okay then. Good.’

‘Sorry about the blank look.’

Sal eased up. He might have smiled.

‘Now don’t get me wrong. It’s not like when the Seans and the Brads come knocking, we’re gonna slam the door in their face. Hell no! We welcome them with open arms. We give them their photo op and we take what they give us. But with all due respect, and I’ll thank you not to quote me on this, they can only take us so far. What we need is Todd Jamison, all the Todd Jamisons we can get our hands on. That, my friend, is how you can help.’

Sal took a deep breath and sighed forcefully. 'Least ways it would sure help yours truly. I just spent half the day sitting in the hot seat making bold optimistic predictions. And in between that I was having to bite my tongue a lot. A lot of people want quick fixes which to them translates to lining their own pockets. They don't want to hear that it's a long process. Debbie may have told you about the meeting.'

'Debbie did tell me. Chamber of Commerce or something like that?'

'Yeah, something like that. Sorry if I was a little over the top just then. Been hitting the hooch a little early today.'

And Sal had just validated Todd's concern. Sal was obviously under a lot of pressure. The only question was from what. He had mentioned that he was going through divorce proceedings but there had to be more to it than that.

'No problem. I never thought of it that way. Thanks for setting me straight. You know you do a pretty good Spook McGillicuddy impersonation.'

'Oh yeah? Who's Spook McGillicuddy?'

'He was my high school basketball coach. You made me realize that I actually kind of miss him.'

'Thanks. I guess. But hey, seems how I'm remembering now that you called this meeting. So what can I do for you?'

'Okay, I've got two things. Item number one concerns where I spend my days. It's getting awkward having to hang out in someone else's office.'

'Glad you brought that up. Monday morning you'll be all set to go. You're gonna be located just behind me. It used to be the janitor's closet. But the good news is it was a spacious janitor's closet. Plus you'll have a back entrance to the private men's room. I've got people coming in over the weekend to fix it all up.'

'Wow. That's awesome. But why such special treatment?'

'For now let's just say I want us to have each other's backs.'

'Okay. Item number two concerns where I spend my nights. I'm taking you up on your offer. I'd like to relocate closer in. Where I'm at is fine. But for an extended stay I need more room. You mentioned a couple of bed and breakfast places the other day. That sounds good. I've gotten used to having breakfast ready when I get up. And with someplace closer in I could walk to work.'

'So you've decided to move out of the Teebow's Motor Court. Have you told Ronnie? I thought she had kinda taken you to raise?'

'Yeah, I haven't told Ronnie yet. But the understanding was I'd stay there just for the week. So the plan is to check out sometime after noon Saturday.'

By now the tension had subsided. Sal was back in the driver's seat being Sal. He was having fun.

'Very well. If that's what you want to do, I highly recommend the Creole Oaks. Nice old place. Very spacious as B and B's go. They love extended stay guests, especially ones I recommend. And it's only a few blocks from right here. Knowing you, you'll probably jog to work everyday. Donny Dulac runs the place. He's an old friend. I'll call him soon as we're done here. He'll be expecting you Saturday afternoon.'

'That was easy enough. Thanks.'
'It's what I do. Now, I've got one thing. I'm a little embarrassed by this but let's talk about a get together for me with Ramona. Nothing formal. Just a chance encounter. A chance to say hello.'

'You mean Ronnie. That's easy. You just come by the motel on Saturday to help me check out and get situated in my new quarters. You're taking a personal interest in this case, right?'

'Hey, nice call. I like that.'

'I have a moment every now and then, in between the blank looks. It'll make things easier for me as well. I've been dreading her reaction when I announce that I'm leaving. She'll probably make another huge sales pitch for me to stay on. All she has to do is look at me with those little girl eyes, call me Cher and I'm powerless. Maybe she really is a fortune teller. But I'm banking that when you show up it'll take her mind completely off that.'

'Oh yeah?'

'Oh yeah. She's still carrying the torch. She didn't make any bones about it.'

'That's the way I remember her. With Ronnie, you always know where you stand.'

'So why are you being so coy? Why don't you just call her or drop by?'

'It wouldn't be prudent what with my divorce still up in the air and all. My wife's lawyer would have a field day. And my lawyer would have a conniption fit. Actually I couldn't care less about that. The real reason is, I want to do this all respectable and proper from a social standpoint. It's a New Orleans thing.'

‘Okay, so why don’t we just go ahead and say 11:00 am tomorrow. You come by and we take it from there. You can play it all nice and innocent. Just let one thing lead to another.’

‘Yeah, and afterwards, when we get you to the Creole Oaks, I can introduce you to Donny, face to face. Make sure he gives you the full treatment.’

‘Sounds like a plan.'

‘Okay good. Now for a little lagniappe. A little birdie told me you have a hot date tonight.’

Todd froze. How did Sal know? What did Sal know?

‘Relax. For what it’s worth, I approve. You’re actually doing me a favor keeping her out of my hair. I have just the place for you to go. Here, take this card and when you get there present it to Clement. So Todd, we good to go?’

‘Good to go, Sal. I feel like I should say ‘Good talk Dad’. I never got to say that.’

Before it even got out of his mouth Todd regretted saying that. Sal nodded. He got it. Todd quickly turned and left without noticing

Chapter 25 - Debbie Cirlot

As Todd walked out of Sal's office Debbie studied him intently. She drank in his every little self conscious mannerism. He hadn't seemed quite so clueless today. There was more purpose in his body language. But something was troubling him. He was obsessing. As he walked out, she got up, went to a filing cabinet and with perfect timing bent over as though to retrieve some documents. Todd couldn't help turning his head and in the process bumped into the doorway. Debbie couldn't help looking up. After an awkward moment of eye contact, he quickly turned and left. Without so much as looking at a folder, she returned to her desk.

Her mind flooded with waves of recrimination. She slumped over and buried her face in her arms. What possessed her to stage that little production? Did she really think it would be cute? Oh god, what must he be thinking of her? She felt tears forming and reached for a tissue. Speaking of obsessing, what the hell was happening to her? The other day when they were discussing Todd, Sal had called her out for blushing. And now there were these tears that came from nowhere.

She might as well admit it. She was attracted to Todd. He was reasonably handsome. Granted he was on the clueless nerdy side but she related to that. She had always been something of a nerd herself. His face was such an open book that she had pretty much been able to size him up from their initial encounter. She felt like she already knew him. Then there was the age difference. But it didn't seem to be a problem with that cutie pie upstairs. Oh yeah, that was all over the building grapevine. Who did they think they were fooling? There was no way that ill fated *pas de deux* was going to last. That little hot pants couldn't wait to get back to Atlanta. Even so, Debbie thought, could she ever hope to break through that clueless barrier? Maybe her mother was right. Maybe she was just unlucky in love. Maybe being smart only made things worse. She reached for another tissue.

Debbie was a native of New Orleans. She grew up in the Gentilly neighborhood and still lived there. Gentilly was unique if not an out and out anomaly. It was middle class or at least as middle class as New Orleans gets. Debbie was exceptionally smart but not a good student. She learned early on that making good grades wasn't popular. She didn't like the other kids teasing her about being a nerd or the teacher's pet. She intentionally underachieved. Nonetheless she was able to coast through high school with a solid B average. That all changed with her freshman year at the University of New Orleans. There she was introduced to more challenging subjects and more inspired teaching.

After earning an undergraduate degree in engineering, she tried interning at a local aeronautics corporation. But corporate life was clearly not for her. Too much politics and backstabbing by people whose only talent was snowing the boss. She decided to continue her education. She'd had enough with high tech studies and turned to the humanities. In two years she earned master's degrees in philosophy and psychology. Next she decided to go for a PHD in psychology. It would not happen.

Being consumed with academics, her social life suffered, which is not to say that it had been that great to begin with. When it came to the opposite sex, Debbie was weird. There was no other way to put it. She was attractive enough but her instincts were all wrong. Relationships would develop and then something deep in her soul would cause her to blow it in the end. And so by the time she reached graduate school, her romantic life had degenerated into a series of casual liaisons with unsuitable guys. Typically they were lonely underclassmen desperate for a date. Something in her identified with them.

It all culminated predictably with an ill timed pregnancy. She decided to keep the baby and dump the daddy. Her schooling thus came to a screeching halt and she was obliged to take any job she could get. She soon learned that, in the job market, a PHD is much better than two MBA's. She was unable to find work in her area of study. Aside from that, there was little or nothing for which she wasn't over qualified. She settled for part time clerical jobs for a couple of years. She didn't mind, it gave her more time with the baby. And with her parents close by she was able to avoid the expense of private day care. Her family supported her throughout the ordeal and that made all the difference for her.

Her big break came after Katrina. Long story short, she ended up working for Sal Leblanc. He was a good boss mostly. He could be demanding but he was also flexible and allowed her time off when home needs required it. He also fast tracked her FEMA grant and made sure that it was more than generous. But she dreamed someday of going to medical school. Someday. In the meantime working for Sal would pay the bills.

Chapter 26 - Dupuy's

As Todd made his way to where he had parked his car, he began to feel steadied by Sal's 'pep talk'. His down river experience now seemed more like an adventure. And he had survived. Sam Dubois had invited him to come back. He even told him that he wasn't as Opie as he looked. That had to be a good thing right? There was still a lot to process but that could wait. Right now he was aching to see Brandi again. He wanted to pour out his heart to her. She likely wouldn't understand the effect it had on him. But as Sal had pointed out, so pointedly, sympathy is overrated. Besides sympathy wasn't what Todd needed. He was looking forward to a romantic rendezvous with a beautiful and intelligent woman.

He hadn't spoken to Brandi since the conference call the day before but they had agreed to meet at a nearby coffee shop at 6pm where he would have the evening planned for them. His frenzied 2 hour trek out and back on St. Charles earlier in the day had left him sweaty and sticky. There was no way he was going in his present state of dishevelment. The evening he had in mind called for jacket and tie. He reckoned he had just enough time to drive to Teebow's, clean up and make it back. Just under two hours later he sat in the coffee shop nursing a cup of French roast. It helped that Ronnie was out running errands when he got there so he didn't have to spend time engaging her. Also he had taken a shortcut that actually ended up being a shortcut.

Todd was anxious. He was no stranger to being stood up. He was elated when Brandi walked in. She didn't care for coffee so they took the trolley as far as Canal street and from there walked into the French Quarter. Brandi announced that she was agreeable with anything the evening had in store. After another long day of being assertive, she was ready to kick back and just go with the flow.

Their first outing had been Brandi's idea of a good evening. The convention hotel restaurant had been glitzy and exciting. Tonight would be a Todd kind of evening. He wanted something traditional and intimate. Sal had told him just the place. Although it was in the French Quarter it was unknown to tourists. The place didn't take reservations but most people in New Orleans liked to dine late. By arriving early they would be able to get a table without a long wait. Sal had also given him a business card on which he scribbled a brief note. When they arrived, he was to show the card to someone named Clement.

They reached Bourbon Street and merged with the summertime tourists. By now it had been closed off to vehicular traffic so everyone trundled happily down the middle of the street. It was major culture shock. Even in his dated cheap suit Todd felt overdressed. For three blocks they navigated their way through a sea of tattoos, denim cut offs, tank tops, and wife beater tee shirts. Then they took a side street that led to an unpromising alley way. Trusting Sal's directions, Todd led them into the alley. They were encouraged by the sight of another well dressed couple in front of them. Following the other couple they reached the end of the alley which opened out into a small courtyard. To the right there was a short line of well heeled patrons who stood outside a door with an elegantly hand painted sign that read 'Dupuy's'.

Again, there was major culture shock. Only this time Todd felt decidedly under dressed. As he took in the decorative ironwork of the old courtyard he imagined all the history that had taken place there. Everything looked at least 200 years old. Jean Lafitte, Jim Bowie, Yancy Derringer, even Andrew Jackson could have frequented this courtyard. Duels of honor were prevalent in the day. Someone might have been shot, knifed, or even hanged in the very spot where he was standing. He was zoning out. Brandi sensed this and gave him a nudge.

Remembering Sal's advice, he resisted the urge to walk in and announce their presence to the host. Instead they took their place in line outside and tried to appear as though they had been there before. Presently a man approached. He wore a crisp white shirt with a black jacket and tie. He regarded them coolly then warmed ever so slightly when he got a better look at Brandi. He politely nodded at her before he spoke.

'Excuse me sir, my name is Clement. I am maître'd here at Dupuy's. I'm familiar with most all of our clientele but I'm afraid you have me at a disadvantage. May I ask who is your waiter?'

'Oh, I'm afraid we don't actually have a waiter. But we're guests of Sal Leblanc. He highly recommended your establishment.'

With that, Todd fumbled for a moment then produced Sal's business card from his coat pocket. Clement looked at the card, read the note scribbled on the reverse and handed it back. He nodded and even managed a brief smile.

'Very good sir. When next you see Mr. Leblanc please give him my warmest regards. There will be just a short wait while we prepare your table. Perhaps you would enjoy a cocktail in the meantime.'

'Dirty Goose for you?' Todd asked Brandi.

She nodded and Todd began to describe a Dirty Goose. Clement interrupted.

'Please sir, Dupuy's practically invented the Dirty Goose. I'm certain it will be to the lady's liking.'

Todd was embarrassed. Brandi was smirking. He needed to say

something. As usual he made it worse.

‘That’s even better. Like we said earlier, we’re just going with the flow. Right, sugar babe?’

Clement looked as if he might laugh but didn’t.

‘And for you sir?’

‘I’ll have me one, I mean I would like a Sazerac.’

‘Excellent sir. I’ll have your cocktails sent right out.’

After Clement left Brandi made no attempt to stifle a snicker.

‘Sugar babe?’

Now she was doubled over. Todd wasn’t so amused.

‘Don’t ask me where that came from?’

’And you were gonna have you one of them Sazeracs. Have you ever lived in Birmingham? I’m sorry a good belly laugh was just what I needed.’

‘Glad I could oblige you.’

Todd looked around. The others waiting in line seemed not to notice. They were absorbed in their own business. He decided to do the same and focus on his dinner companion. It wasn’t hard to do. Brandi looked stunning and was enjoying herself albeit at his expense. It helped immensely when a cocktail waiter brought their drinks. After that first blessed sip he thought, there must be 50 ways to embarrass yourself around a younger woman.

‘So tell me about your day,’ Todd asked.

‘Well the big thing you’ll be interested in is feedback from the conference call, the conference call from hell as you dubbed it. Based on the information from my unimpeachable source, you were well received.’

‘That’s a pleasant surprise.’

‘Sanford the senior partner was impressed with your testimony that I wrote for you. And you read it quite well I should say. That was the deciding factor. The partners think you’re the right man for the job.’

‘No negative comments? Surely there were some.’

‘Just the usual office politics. One of my rivals tried to cast you in a bad light but that was seen for what it was. It was a dig at me not you. So congratulations, you passed. Cheers.’

‘Something tells me that you might be sugar coating it. But I’ll drink to that. Now let me tell you about my day. Are you familiar with the term broke dick dog?’

Brandi’s expression clearly said she was not. Todd began to elaborate on his experience including the blow by blow he’d gotten from Sam Dubois. Just as he expected, Brandi was interested but clueless as to the emotional impact of it all. Never mind, it was good just to unload it on someone. A few minutes later, Clement reappeared and informed them that their table was ready. He led them past the raised eyebrows of the others who were waiting in line. The relatively plain exterior gave no clue as to what to expect on the inside. It was much larger than expected and lavish. It was overwhelming. Once inside Clement signaled and the table waiter appeared.

‘Allow me to introduce Robin. He will be your server. However if I may be of service in any way, do not hesitate to let me know.'

After Clement excused himself, Robin spoke.

'Welcome to Dupuy's. I understand that this is your first time with us.'

Todd nodded.

'Why don't I let you enjoy your drinks while you have a look at the menu? I'll come back in a few minutes to answer any questions you may have.'

'The menu is in French?' Todd noted.

Robin was gracious. 'Yes, I'll be glad to explain it all to you.'

'That won't be necessary,' Todd replied.

Brandi gave him a questioning look.

'No problem, I took French in high school.'

After a few minutes Robin returned and could see that they were still mystified by the menu.

Todd explained, 'It's not the French. It's just that this font makes some of the words hard to make out.'

Brandi snickered and hid her face. Robin pretended not to notice.

'Of course, monsieur. I have a suggestion. And I should mention that it's what many of our long time customers like to do. If I may point to your menu, you see this entree that is called 'l'envie du jour'. It is basically Dupuy's version of, how shall I say, of the blue plate special. But it is unlike any blue plate special you may have had before. Perhaps that would be satisfactory.'

Brandi approved. 'That sounds awesome to me. We're just going with the flow tonight. Right, sugar babe?'

Todd winced.

'That will be fine.'

'Excellent monsieur. And might I also recommend a bottle of champagne to make the evening even more special.'

'Yeah sure.'

Todd wondered how much is this going to cost.

'Shall I bring you a wine list sir?'

Todd freaked out sort of, then recovered, sort of. Not knowing if there was such a thing, he declared, 'Uh no. We'll do the 'l'envie du jour' champagne.'

Robin remained gracious.

'I think I get your drift sir. I'll bring one of my personal favorites. I am sure you will find it satisfactory.'

A few minutes later the lights dimmed. Being all too familiar with old wiring, Todd's first thought was that a circuit breaker had tripped. To his surprise, Robin appeared with a bottle of champagne, two crystal stemmed glasses and a silver ice bucket. Then the lights came back up. Suddenly their table was the center of attention. This made Todd uncomfortable but Brandi was digging it big time. Robin showed the bottle to Todd who ritually nodded in approval. The cork was expertly popped and the two crystal glasses were filled with an effervescence that never seemed to stop.

From that point they sat and watched as a true haute cuisine dining experience unfolded before them. As good as the food was, it was even more about production and presentation with Robin orchestrating the whole dazzling affair. There were first courses followed by second courses followed by a simple salad. Next came a plate offering a choice of cheeses.

The meal was ended with something called cafe brulot. Robin was disappointed when they declined to have dessert. But he was insistent that they allow him to prepare this classic New Orleans after dinner drink. Cafe brulot was a concoction of strong coffee, strong liquor and heady spices prepared table side in a highly ornate silver service bowl. Once again the lights were dimmed for dramatic effect. The liquor and coffee were mixed and then set aflame while Robin stirred it up with a silver ladle producing flames a foot high. He intentionally spilled some onto the heavy white tablecloth producing a harmless but pretty blue flame. The ladle was made in the shape of a gargoyle's head. In good time the still flaming mixture was ladled from the bowl and poured through the gargoyle's open mouth into demitasse cups. It was high drama that ended the meal perfectly and left them with an exquisite buzz.

In the end Todd thanked Robin for a special evening. He asked to speak to Clement and thanked him as well. Clement personally showed them out and wished them a good evening. When they had left, the maitre'd and his best waiter discussed the unique pleasure of showing off their establishment to newcomers.

'Did you see their faces, especially when you were preparing the cafe brulot?' Clement asked. 'You completely blew them away. Due to our limited clientele, it is something that we do not get to experience nearly enough. That is unfortunate.'

Robin agreed.

'It was my pleasure as well.'

Clement looked a bit puzzled. 'You know as I walked them out, he had a most interesting comment. He said 'the reconciliation of opposites is not for wimps'. What do you suppose that could mean?'

Robin shook his head.

'Who knows? Who cares? So do you think he will be lucky tonight?'

Clement grinned a thoughtful grin.

'I think he's lucky no matter what. The girl is more than beautiful. She is intelligent as well. I couldn't help but notice that he spoke at great length, pouring his heart out about something and she listened with interest. That is the mark of a true lady.'

Robin nodded in agreement.

'Perhaps he was explaining how the reconciliation of opposites is not for wimps.'

Clement chuckled.

'Well you certainly did right by them and then some. My compliments on your service tonight. We always want to do our best for friends of Sal Leblanc.'

'Thank you. And I cut them some slack on the bill as you requested. I didn't realize that Sal Leblanc had so much influence here at Dupuy's.'

Clement was kind in his reproach, 'Maybe someday when you are maître'd you will understand. It is not about influence. It is about friendship.'

Chapter 27 - Savoir Faire is Overrated

Clement had showed Todd and Brandi out through a different door than the one they entered. It avoided the alley and conveniently put them out on a side street near Bourbon. It was actually the original front door. It would have been possible to enter the restaurant this way. Those who tried, however, would be met by a smiling receptionist who would inform them that the restaurant was booked solid for the evening, which was the truth. Only in New Orleans.

Todd and Brandi walked back toward Bourbon Street arm in arm leaning into each other for support and feeling a considerable warm glow from their dining experience. Bourbon street seemed less emasculating than it had earlier. It was, however, still wall to wall tourists so they negotiated their way across it and continued down to the next street which was Royal. It was considerably less crowded and quieter.

'The night is still young,' Todd observed. 'We can go left to the other end of Royal if you like. As I remember there are some cool antique shops. Or we can head back.'

Brandi lost her balance and grabbed Todd with both arms.

'Woops, I vote for heading back.'

'That's good. I'm kind of walked out anyway.'

'I would hope so after this afternoon. By the way, thanks for an unbelievable evening. Not that it's over, necessarily.'

'You can thank Sal for recommending the restaurant. It was unbelievable, in more ways than one. Granted the sugar babe faux pas happened. But after that things went a lot smoother. I feel like I got into a rhythm.'

Brandi rolled her eyes as best she could in her state of intoxication.

'Actually the sugar babe faux pas as you call it was one of my favorite parts. It's what I like about you. When you open your mouth, I never know what's going to come out.'

'You swear? It's been my experience that girls don't like that about me.'

'Well guess what, some girls do. But I can see what you're saying. A lot of people just don't get you, Beave.'

'Beave? You were calling me that the other night.'

'Beats the hell out of Gomer.'

He laughed.

'Hey, I just found out today that I'm not as Opie as I look. But seriously folks, I think I showed some *savoir faire* back there. I think French restaurants might just be my thing.'

'Whatever, if that makes you happy. Me, I say *savoir faire* is overrated. I mean all day long I'm drowning in a sea of measured responses and well considered positions. Anything creative is anathema. A little spontaneous is what floats my boat.'

It's true he thought. In her position she didn't get to let her hair down that often. Enough with the words. What is she really telling me? The day's events had emboldened him. He stopped and turned to face her.

'How's this for a little spontaneous.'

He embraced her and they kissed. It was not a polite kiss but rather desperate and angst filled. He surprised himself. And Brandi surprised herself. Neither reluctant nor eager, she accepted it with perfect surrender. She was a compliant, cleaving noodle. They continued until she broke it off.

Before speaking, she took a moment to catch her breath.

'So I take it you're still good with this arrangement? No misgivings from the other night?'

'Right now I know exactly what I want.'

And Brandi knew exactly what she wanted. All of a sudden she seemed less tipsy. She kicked off her heels and proceeded to walk in stocking feet.

'Okay, so let's pick up the pace. I'll give you another tour of my place. I'm guessing you don't remember too much from the other night.'

'You're right. Maybe you could show me your baseball glove again.'

The trolley ride back to Terpsichore HQ seemed to take forever. From there they drove in separate cars back to Brandi's house. The promised tour was completely forgotten. Todd was aching for this moment. During the meal he had talked about his down river experience and how it had gotten inside his head. Brandi listened and was sympathetic but just couldn't fathom what he was talking about. It was only when they kissed back on Royal Street that she began to understand. And when they became intimate she totally got it. He was more serious, more sure of himself. He was on fire.

When their passion was spent, they collapsed into a brief semi-conscious nap. A few minutes later when they were awake again Todd decided to make an announcement.

‘I have some news. I’m moving tomorrow. I’ll be walking distance from my office, and from here.’

‘That’s very cool. So why did you wait until now to tell me?’

‘Well until now I wasn't sure you would think it was a good thing.’

‘Of course I do. It should simplify the ‘stay or go’ issue, which we still haven’t settled by the way. I honestly don’t know what the big deal is. Were you thinking of staying tonight?’

‘Some other time. I know I promised to make you coffee and all and I will. There’s just too much to do in the morning. I have to be out before noon. But we could do something in the afternoon. I could show you my new place. You could help me get set up. We could go for a run. I hear Audubon Park is nice.’

‘No can do, Beave. I have a morning flight to Atlanta tomorrow.’

‘When will you be back?’

‘Not until Tuesday evening. There’s a big get together Monday, a command performance. We’re meeting with a German consulting firm who represent one of the big auto companies. They’re looking to build an assembly plant somewhere in the southeast. We’re partnering with them to find a suitable location. We’ll be putting our best foot forward. I even get to give a presentation on what TGG is doing here. It will be an all day affair. Of course, we’ll wine and dine them that evening. Then Tuesday morning we’ll see them off. After that there’s a follow up meeting with the partners to assess how things went. Then a late afternoon flight

back. I should be
arriving at Louis Armstrong around 7 pm Tuesday.'

'So the meeting is not until Monday. Why are you leaving tomorrow?'

'Family, friends. I still have a life there you know.'

Todd was crestfallen. He had hoped to spend at least some of the weekend with Brandi.

'Do we know each other well enough for me to say I'll miss you?'

'Probably not. But you can say it anyway. I haven't left yet. You can stay a while tonight can't you?'

Todd had to agree. He felt stupid for asking. But he still wasn't looking forward to being alone for the weekend. It was his first week end away from Memphis.

She got up and slipped on a just barely long enough designer tee shirt. She went into the kitchen and returned with two glasses of white wine. They lay there and listened to one of her favorite CD's.

Todd should have been contented but instead he was distracted and restless. He found her music annoying. At least the wine was good. They conversed at length, but the things they talked about only seemed to underscore their age and lifestyle differences. Brandi seemed not to notice. She had what she wanted. She was enjoying the moment as well as anticipating the weekend in Atlanta. As the cafe brulot wore off she became sleepy. After she stifled a yawn, Todd excused himself and wished her safe travel.

As he drove back to Teebow's he thought about Brandi and how amazing she looked tonight. The evening couldn't have been more perfect and yet he had been anxious to leave her place. At the same time he rued the fact that she would be gone for the next few days. Mick Jagger missed the point. It's not that you can't always get what you want. It's more like getting what you want doesn't make you happy. But not having it still makes you unhappy. He was bemused by the illogic of what he was feeling. Why hadn't he felt this way the other night? For one thing he had been considerably more plastered. And he had passed out. There's that. Having thus confronted one of the basic issues of existence, his mind settled into a kind of mellow existential funk.

Chapter 28 - When Ronnie met Sally

Todd slept well. He pretty much collapsed as soon as he hit the bed. The previous day, hell, the whole week had given him a lot to sleep on. He woke at the usual time then remembered it was Saturday. He tried sleeping in but gave up after lying awake for an hour. He took his time cleaning up and getting dressed.

By 10:00 am he was in the motel dining room drinking coffee and trying to read the local paper. He was barely able to skim the headlines. Foremost in his mind was how to tell Ronnie he was moving to a new hotel. Ronnie emerged from the small kitchen with a platter full of breakfast. Todd smiled in response and dug in.

‘So you like my cooking don’t you? I’ve been feeding you good these last few days. What’s it been a week now?’

‘Almost. It was last Sunday night when I walked through that door looking for a room, for one night. That was some sales job you put on me.’

‘And the rest is history, eh Cher? I’m telling you, you were a pretty sad sack when you walked in here that night. You looked like you needed a friend.’

She laughed.

‘And you had money. You didn’t think I’d let you go after just one night did you? Now look at you. You’re looking all perked up. Okay you may be a little hung over. But you’re learning your way around. You’ve had a big week, a good week I think.’

‘And for that I owe you big time. I’ll never be able to...’

‘Yeah, yeah, yeah. You had the potential; you just needed a little coaching. I could see that right off the bat.’

Now was as good a time as any to take the plunge.

‘Well be that as it may, I’ll be checking out today. I know my 7 days aren’t up yet but it’s Sal’s idea. He wants me closer in. Says the higher ups are taking a real interest in my case. I’m kind of like the poster child or the guinea pig, I guess.’

Todd braced for Ronnie to react. She didn’t disappoint him.

‘Oh Cher, what’s the matter? I ain’t been taking good enough care of you? You getting tired of my home cooked breakfast every morning?’

‘You know better than that. It was just a matter of time before I moved anyway.’

‘Yeah, it’s just that you seemed different, special in some way I can’t describe. You showed up here for some reason. Everything happens for a reason.’

‘Hey, I feel the same way. You’re the first person I met here. You’re the first friend I made here. Me spending the week here wasn’t just a business decision. It was more than that. I was a stranger and you took me in. I don’t take that for granted, not for one second. It has been a special week and I don’t want to lose that. I want us to stay in touch.’

‘Yeah, yeah, yeah. Right. Nice try.’

Todd realized he was laying it on too thick. Ronnie was feeling patronized.

‘Okay. We can fight this out til the cows come home if you like.’

He paused to look at his watch.

'But it will have to be some other time. Sal's coming by at 11 o'clock to help me move.'

Sal was the ace in the hole and Todd had played his hole card perfectly.

'Sal Leblanc is coming? Why didn't you say so? 11 o'clock? That's 30 minutes from now. I need to do some things. Just serve yourself. You know where everything is.'

Ronnie got up and walked through the office into her apartment. Todd refilled his cup and continued trying to read the paper. Eventually he became interested in an article about the post Katrina recovery. The piece went into some detail about allegations of kickbacks and misappropriation of FEMA funds. He became engrossed to the point that he was caught unawares when Sal entered.

'Am I interrupting anything?' Sal asked.

Todd got up but before he could speak Ronnie appeared as if on cue. Todd couldn't believe his eyes. She was carrying a silver service of freshly made coffee. More incredibly she had put on fresh makeup. She was wearing a dress that, except for the apron, seemed more suited to evening than morning. She looked ten years younger. She was hot.

Ronnie carefully laid the coffee service on one of the tables and turned to face Sal. It was obvious that they recognized each other but there was a protocol that must be followed. The ruse was on. Todd of course was clueless to all this. She waited a moment for Todd to make introductions. When he said nothing she spoke.

'So Todd, who is our guest?'

‘Oh, Ronnie this is Sal Leblanc who I spoke to you about. He’s been helping me get settled here. In fact he’s here today to uh, to help me get relocated to a different place.’

Ronnie offered her hand.

‘How do you do Mr. Leblanc?’

‘Please, it’s Sal. I’m quite fine thank you.’

‘Strangest thing, I used to know a Sal Leblanc in school way back when. He was just about the most handsome guy in the whole school. He would have known me as Ramona Chauvin.’

‘I do indeed remember a girl named Ramona, quite fondly I might add. And I would be that same Sal Leblanc, at your service. My dearest friends have always called me Sally. I would like it if you called me that as well.’

‘Very well, Sally. And the Ramona Chauvin you remember was an innocent sheltered little girl. I’ve done some growing up since then and I’m not so innocent anymore. I’m Ronnie now.’

‘Yeah, I was just noticing that. Okay, Ronnie it is.’

At some point, Todd realized that he had become invisible. He excused himself to deaf ears and left to load up the hatchback.

‘So Sally, I only learned a few minutes ago that you were coming. I’m afraid you’ve caught me unprepared to receive company. All I can offer you is some fresh hand poured coffee.’

‘That would be nice. Nothing like hand poured coffee. What with all the fancy programmable coffee makers, it’s a lost art anymore.’

After they had savored a few sips of the aromatic brew, the formal conversation became more direct and personal.

'Tell me Sally, what have you been up to lately? Where have you been all my life?'

Sal squirmed a bit and then chuckled. 'Hello. Nothing like cutting to the chase. You haven't changed much, have you?'

'It's the only way I know how to be.'

'Fair enough. I'll try to keep it brief. After we got out of school I was advised I should go to college. So I went to UNO for one term and dropped out. It just wasn't for me. Plus I was broke and family money was tight. I needed to get a job. After looking around for a while my Dad called a few friends and I end up working for a chauffeur service. I liked it. I learned early on that if you respect yourself and take pride in what you do, people will respect you. Actually, I didn't like it, I loved it. I loved driving a big fancy car, still do. I loved taking important people all over town to all the fine hotels and restaurants. Commander's, Galatoire's, the Roosevelt, the Monteleone, it was seriously nice. And I got to know the people who worked in those places: the head waiters, the maitre'd's, the concierges. It made me feel important. Plus it put me in a position to do favors for my clients. Evidently they took a liking to me and it led to better things. And now here I am working for FEMA, in charge of rebuilding this city.'

As Sal reminisced he teared up a little.

'You know, this city is one of the loves of my life. Yesterday I was reading a report from one of our consulting firms. We've lost nearly two-thirds of our people. They project that in five years we'll barely be back to half our original population. Tell me, Ronnie. What's happened to our lovely town? Will we ever put her back together?'

'Sure you will Sally. A town is its people. As long as there's people like you our town will survive.'

'And as long as there's people like you.'

After a blush, Ronnie spoke.

'So tell me about your family.'

'Well, I'm afraid that part of my life hasn't worked out too well.'

'Any children?'

'Just one, a son. After him Mrs. Leblanc didn't care to go through that again.'

'But you're Catholic and she is too, right? You don't believe in...'

Sal's face hardened showing a deep disgust.

'We used the same birth control as a priest. Abstinence.'

Sal caught himself.

'What am I saying? Please excuse me. I'm not myself lately, tearing up like this and speaking so rudely.'

'It's okay Sally.' She reached out and touched his hand. 'You can always tell me your deepest feelings.'

And it was as though the years they had been apart melted away. This produced more tears which he quickly wiped away.

'Not a word of this to Jamison you understand.'

‘Mum’s the word. So you have a son. Tell me about him.’

‘He’s doing fine, from what I hear. He’s a real bright kid, like his old man. Unlike his old man, he was an ‘A’ student. So we sent him to a good school in the East. He did well there. He liked it so much he stayed. Still not married. He comes down for Mardi Gras and Christmas. Mostly to hang out with friends. We barely see him even then. Oh yeah, and I’m in the process of getting a divorce. There’s that.’

‘Oh Sally I’m sorry to hear?’

Ronnie feared she might have sounded less than sincere. Sal seemed not to notice. He was interested in hearing her story.

‘And that’s it, all short and sweet. Now it’s your turn.’

‘During school I dated around a good bit, but nothing serious. After school my family wanted me to go to college. One of my uncles on my mother’s side lived in Lafayette. He wanted me to go to the university there. And since he was willing to foot a good bit of the bill, that’s what I did. Besides that, I wanted to get away. There just wasn’t a whole lot to keep me here. At least that was my thinking at the time.’

‘Perhaps I should blame...’

‘Save it. You’re flattering yourself.’

Sal sputtered, chuckled, then recovered.

‘So your mother’s family is Acadian?’

‘Cajuns, Sally. Pure dee and proud of it.’

‘I should have known that when we were in school together.

Guess I forgot.'

'I never talked about it. Guess I didn't want people to know what with the jokes and all. School kids can be really mean. But in case you haven't figured it out, I'm over it now.'

'So how was it at Southwest Louisiana?'

'It was a completely different world. Funny how what goes around comes around. People in Lafayette hated New Orleans. So after all those years of hiding the fact that my mother's family was Acadian, now I'm hiding the fact that I'm from New Orleans. It served me right. I learned my lesson.

'Then I met this nice guy from Breaux Bridge, Kieran Geracie. And could he dance. He was a dancing fool. There was so much more to him than that but the dancing is what sticks in my mind. Guess it's the Cajun in me. We were both smitten. He proposed and I accepted. By then I had lost all interest in school. I was getting homesick. He knew I was a New Orleans girl at heart. God bless him, he was willing to move. He had some family money and so did I. We bought this place and fixed it up a bit. We named it for my mother. Her maiden name is Thibaut. We changed the spelling to Teebow's so tourists would know how to pronounce it. I've been here ever since.'

Sal hesitated then spoke.

'Todd mentioned that you were a widow. If you don't mind me asking, what happened to....?'

'I don't mind. We weren't making enough from the motor court to start a family so he started doing work on the side. Oil rigs in the gulf and the Atchafalaya basin. He had studied engineering at Lafayette but didn't get his degree. So he started at the bottom.

He was good at it. It soon became his full time job. He worked his way up to safety inspector. The money was good. But he was staying gone more and more, traveling from rig to rig. I got pretty good at running this place by myself. He was good to call me every night.

'One day I got a call from one of the oil company executives. There was an explosion on the drilling platform where he was doing a safety inspection of all things. The whole crew was killed. I was devastated of course. They never determined the cause of the explosion. Could have been some doofus was dying for a cigarette and lit up. There was a settlement. It helped some. But I had to sell our house and live here full time. I kept this place and scraped by as best I could. Of course my family offered to let me live with them. They fairly begged me to. But once you been on your own you can't go back home. This was all I knew to do. I kept Teebow's going and it's kept me going. I've gotten by.'

'I'm so sorry to hear about that. So no kids?'

'We never got around to it. He was in line for a promotion where he wouldn't be gone all the time. We were waiting for that then the accident happened.'

'So how is it that a lady such as you is alone? Or am I assuming too much?'

'No no. I'm afraid you're looking at it.'

'I certainly am. But you must have still been pretty young. Did you ever have any interest in remarrying? Or did you just feel like no one else could ever do?'

Ronnie was blushing again.

'Oh I felt that way for a while but you gradually you get over it.

Time does that. I was open to a new start, but running Teebow's isn't exactly conducive to having an active social life. Another thing time does is get away from you. One day I wake up to find I'm a middle aged widow. But I'm basically alright with that. I have my routine. It keeps me busy. You meet some interesting people.

'And it's not like I'm stuck here all the time. When business is slow, I'll close up for a couple of weeks and spend some time with family, do a little traveling with friends. Actually, I had planned to do that this week. Then Todd Jamison walks in asking for a room for the night. I figure he was just another drifter looking to hustle some Katrina money. You know the type?'

'Jesus, Mary and Holy Joseph, you have no idea. You're preaching to the choir.'

'Yeh well, I was dismissive, even a little rude to him at first. But then after taking a good look at him something softened in me. He seemed so lost, so clueless.'

'Yeah, I know that look.'

'And of all the places he could've stayed he chooses Teebow's. I took an interest in him for no reason that makes any sense. Plus he did have money. So he ends up taking a room for the week and now here you are. The other day when he mentioned your name, that's when it hit me. I've been good as dead for all these years.'

Now it was her time to tear up. Sal quickly offered her his handkerchief.

'Everything happens for a reason, Ronnie. Or so they say.'

'I do believe in that. So much has happened this week. It's the first time I've felt alive in years. But I'm afraid of where this might lead. The changes it might bring. I was comfortable in my humdrum routine. Oh dear, now I'm the one who's assuming too much.'

'You're assuming correctly. I did want to see you. That's the real reason I'm sitting here having this conversation. I realize I may have come on a little strong by just popping in here barely announced. For that I apologize.'

'You haven't changed much either, Sally.'

Sal reached out and took Ronnie by both hands.

'You're even more beautiful than I remembered. Yeah, I totally forgot. And when I look into your eyes I still see a teenage girl in there. I still see Ramona.'

They stood up. Sal moved closer, she moved closer, they embraced. They almost kissed. Then their passion gave way to embarrassment. Sal backed off and tried to speak. He cleared his throat.

'I'm sorry for that.'

'Sorry for what?'

'I've always been sort of a control freak. I wasn't prepared for how I'm feeling right now. We need to obey the speed limit. Besides the divorce I've got other business to tend to as well. As far as the rest of the world is concerned, I'm just here going the extra mile to help a project applicant.'

'I'm sure you know what's best, but for the record I'm not sorry.'

'Yeah well, for the record, noted.'

‘I’m serious Sally, you can call me anytime. With Todd gone I’ll have a lot of time on my hands. My schedule is completely open, and so am I.’

‘Speaking of, I’m thinking our boy wonder is probably loaded up by now. Hey, what was that silly thing we use to say? I’ll be in tow?’

‘A bientot, Sally.’

After Sal left, Ronnie felt flushed and faint. She took a seat and began to cry but it was more from a release of joy than sadness.

Chapter 29 - Donny Dulac

Todd followed Sal to his new residence, the Creole Oaks Inn. It was located in the Lower Garden District on Melpomene Street. He had chosen it because it was just a few blocks from Terpsichore HQ where his new office would be located. It was also just a few blocks from Brandi's house in the Garden District, happy coincidence that. The Inn itself was pretty much as Sal had described it, an Italianate style two story mansion similar in style to Terpsichore HQ. Like that building it had once been a private residence. It had now been restored and converted into a bed and breakfast, a rather grand one at that. It was larger than most and could accommodate up to 15 guests. True to its name the Creole Oaks Inn was flanked by giant live oak trees that framed the entrance and ran the length of the property.

The proprietor was Donny Dulac who, big surprise, just happened to be a good friend of Sal's. Donny seemed agreeable and easy going. He liked to joke and kid which reminded Todd of the exchange he had with Ed Segura at the Segway's Pit Stop earlier in the week. Sal made introductions then took Donny aside and explained all the financial arrangements. Todd was given one of the so called VIP suites on the second floor. There was a bedroom with an adjoining bath. The living area included a kitchenette and a small refrigerator. Donny opened the door to the refrigerator to reveal a complimentary six pack of Dixie beer. There were French doors that opened out onto a private balcony that overlooked Melpomene street. Nice place to sit it out until his house was livable. Why would he ever want to leave here, he thought. You could always count on Sal to come through for you.

After Sal left, Donny wanted to talk. In particular, he wanted to talk about Sal. Something about the way Donny put it drew Todd's attention. Donny suggested they go out to the balcony.

Todd agreed. It was after 12 noon on a Saturday which is cocktail hour in the Big Easy. Anticipating a lengthy conversation, Todd grabbed a cold beer from the refrigerator. He offered one to Donny who declined. Out on the balcony there was shade and a nice breeze. It was warm but not oppressive.

Todd took a sip.

'Ah, very nice. I'm developing a taste for Dixie.'

Donny was not a big fan of flattery but Todd seemed genuine. He smiled.

'Yeah well, we do what we can. I'm glad to see you making yourself at home already. So you like our beer? It's made here local you know.'

'I like everything about your place, Donny. I know this is supposed to be temporary, but I'm wondering why I'd ever want to leave.'

'You're welcome to stay a week, 6 months, a year, however long you want.'

'Thanks. Really nice and quiet up here. It's kind of a mad house downstairs though. Is it like that all the time?'

'Yeah, I ain't complaining neither. Business is good. There's been a steady stream of people from out-of-town to help rebuild the city. Contractors from Houston. Consultants from Atlanta. You'd think with all the homeless people there'd be a lot of residential contractors right? Wrong. It's been mostly business contractors and advertising consultants. The first order of construction was to fix the roof on the Superdome. And now the city is spending a fortune on developing an ad campaign that will get the tourists back. That's all Huey's doing you understand.'

'So who is Huey?'

'That's Huey Fitzgerald, he's Sal's boss. Sorry, I guess I figured Sal would have mentioned that.

'So all Huey can think about is getting the tourists back. Eventually though, with Sal's persistent urging, they start to think about the citizens or ex citizens as the case may be. It's like, oh yeah, maybe we need to figure out a way to get people to move back and actually live here?'

'You said they? Who exactly are 'they'?'

Donny made a polite chuckle.

'Huey calls the shots but he gets a lot of helpful advice from the local interests on how to do his job. That's who 'they' are. Naturally that all flows down to Sal and the other neighborhood directors.'

He cleared his throat.

'Which brings us to what I actually wanted to talk to you about. I've known Sal since our school days. He's as good a friend as I have in the world. Without him I'd still be standing in line in the hot sun trying to get a small business grant from FEMA. Take a look around. As you can see, I got a pretty nice gig here huh?'

'Preachin' to the choir, Donny. I've just spent the last six months sitting all day in every employment office in Memphis. Without Sal I'd still be there, getting turned down for various and sundry reasons.'

'Sal told me you were from Memphis. So did you know Elvis?'

Todd started to respond.

'No I'm kidding. Sorry. Let me try to be serious for a minute. Now Sal he may be all cool and collected on the outside, but I tell you inside he's a ticking time bomb.'

'I've sensed that. He's made a few vague comments to me about having some problems with his higher ups. I've noticed he keeps a pint of brandy in his desk.'

'You don't know the half of it. Think about it. There is all this federal money up for grabs and not a lot of accountability. That's a classic recipe for ugly politics. Now Sal, he thinks top priority should be given to individuals who have lost their homes and to the smaller businesses. On the other hand, the interests favor a 'trickle down' approach. The theory being that you seed the money up top and from there the money will trickle down to where it's needed. As you might imagine, there's a lot of support for this approach from those at the top.'

Todd figured he was supposed to laugh and did. Donny continued.

'You laugh but that's always been the way things get done around here. Go along, get along. All the other neighborhood directors are playing ball. Sal is all that stands in the way. You see Katrina changed a lot of things and Sal is thinking it's time for the old way of doing business to change.

'So Sal, he's paid his dues. He commands a lot of respect with the interests. He's managed to sway their thinking some. This Terpsichore Project that he masterminded really helped. At first everyone was skeptical of it. They really thought Sal had lost his mind. But after the FEMA brass gave it the okay everyone's taking credit for it. So Sal's a big hero, for a while. But you know how it is. It's always what have you done for me lately. Plus the damage had already been done. He managed to ruffle some pretty important feathers. That's why I'm concerned about him. It's even costing him his marriage.'

'You swear? I mean I knew he was getting a divorce. Just didn't know any of the details.'

'Chartreuse, that's his wife, she thinks he's gone nuts. Real piece of work, that one. One of the Duvachez clan from up Natchez. Classic examples of Mississippi barefoot aristocrats. Old family, old money, but seeing hard times of late. She thought she was marrying some hot political rock star, not some David who's gonna take on Goliath. She sees all this as a threat to their livelihood which is to say her livelihood. Now she's looking to cut her losses and get while the gettin's good. Even as we speak their lawyers are duking it out over the financial settlements. And if I know Chartreuse, she's probably got somebody waiting in the wings.'

Todd shook his head.

'Been there done that myself.'

'So you know what I'm talking about, what he's going through.'

'Yeah, a little bit. I've been through a divorce. It really wasn't all that bad.'

'Yeah well Sal's is. He doesn't make many mistakes. But marrying that out-of-towner was a big one. Mind you that's one man's opinion. I'll thank you not to quote me on that, or anything else we've talked about.'

‘Not a problem. But Sal strikes me as a ‘go along, get along’ kind of guy. And I’ve seen him in action. He is a rock star.’

‘Normally that’s exactly what he is.’

‘So why is he doing this?’

‘Like I said earlier, Katrina was a game changer. After the mass evacuation he went a little nuts. The streets were inaccessible so he hires a private helicopter. Every day for two weeks he flies over, surveying the devastation. I’m talking Jefferson, Orleans, St. Bernard, Plaquemine, every friggin’ parish. Seeing it all up close was a ‘road to Damascus’ experience for him. He’s always said that this town is the love of his life only now it’s in spades. He’s a different animal. He’s very passionate about doing what he thinks is best for his town. So much so that he’s willing to risk his career. You know, a lot of people think he’s right. They agree with his approach. And needless to say, a lot of people don’t.’

‘Okay. Why are you telling me this? How does this affect me?’

‘Oh it definitely affects you. I’m trying to give a heads up on the situation, for Sal’s sake and yours. He’s liable to be a little touchy now and then. So don’t take it personally. Also he might need a little favor from you some day. If it comes to that, he’ll expect you to do it.’

‘Uh? Yeah, sure thing, Donny. No problem.’

‘Word to the wise, Todd. Sal can be your best friend or your worst enemy. Don’t ever forget that. But you should know he speaks well of you. That’s saying something. Generally he doesn’t think much of out-of-towners. Guess I better leave you with that. I’m all talked out anyways. I’m gonna be kinda scarce til after church tomorrow afternoon. It’s fixing to be Saturday night in New Orleans. Got a hot date with the missus. There's a big fundraiser dance at Elmwood. But if you need anything just let the front desk know. I'll make sure they know who you are. And one last thing, this conversation never took place. I'm outta here.'

As Donny left, he was hoping he hadn't said too much. Sal had put him up to this. Just don't mention any names Sal had told him.

Chapter 30 - Running Home to Mama

It took all of an hour for Todd to get his things unloaded and arranged to his liking. He felt tired. He flopped on the bed and tried to take a nap. No way. His mind was staccato restless. He could scarcely remember anything he and Donny had talked about. It had been a busy week. He had been faced with new experiences nonstop from the Old Señor to Brandi Mendelssohn to the Broke Dick Dog district. Somehow he had dealt with all those new experiences. Now it was the weekend. He was faced with an old familiar nemesis that had plagued him ever since his divorce. He was faced with time on his hands.

And it would prove to be his undoing. Brandi was gone. Ronnie was gone. Sal was gone. And it was quiet, way too quiet. He felt those magnificent, high ceilinged walls closing in on him. Angst at fifty, long a subject of wry humor, was suddenly too real to be funny. He reached for his guitar but just couldn't seem to get it in tune. Nothing he played sounded right. He tried going for a walk. That was too slow. He tried running but he quickly became winded. It was too hot, too late in the day and he'd just had a beer. After a block he turned around. He decided to jump in the hatchback. It was a small oasis of familiarity. It felt good to be driving. He drove to Arabi to Sam's pool hall. He might feel welcome there. Sam was out. He ordered a cold beer. Camilla was there. She remembered him from the other day but beyond that Todd was unable to make any conversation. She was too busy anyway. A tour bus had just dropped in. He gulped down the beer then left. He just needed to be moving. He pointed the hatchback north and went running home to mama.

Six hours later Todd found himself in midtown Memphis. He stopped at a convenience store to gas up, pee, and purchase a quart of beer. He was possessed by a strange and relentless energy so he kept driving. Driving around the old stomping grounds. Driving past all the familiar, memorable spots, nursing his quart. Never stopping except to pee and purchase another quart. It was just like old times except it wasn't. It all seemed foreign and dreamlike. It was true what the poet said. Women do seem wicked when you're unwanted. It never occurred to him that he was running a high risk of getting pulled over. Luckily that didn't happen. When at long last he had exhausted himself, he found a motel and barely made it to his room before crashing.

Chapter 31 - My Dinner with Alex

The next morning he woke up hungover but restless. How long had he been out? He checked his watch. It was almost noon. He hadn't slept in that late since college. Not taking time to clean up, he hastily checked out then went straight to the mini warehouse where his belongings were stored. In his new Creole Oaks residence he would have room for a few more things: books, CD's, stereo, headphones, more clothes. After loading the hatchback he thought what else could he do here? Then he realized there was nowhere to go. There was nothing to do but drive back to New Orleans. As he gassed up, he thought to check his oil level. The hatchback was two quarts low so he topped it off and said a little prayer that all would be well on the trip back. He decided to grab something to eat before he left.

He had just pulled out of a Krystal and was making his way to the interstate. Just before he reached the entry ramp he spotted a hitchhiker. As he got closer something about the face looked vaguely familiar. Was this someone he knew from school? After the previous evening he wasn't sure he could trust his eyes. It wasn't a good place to be on foot. He pulled over and beckoned to the hitcher who promptly got in.

'Thanks for the ride man.'

'No problem. Not the best part of town to be on foot. What are you doing out here anyway?'

The hitcher shrugged, 'It's as far as my last ride took me.'

Then it hit him. 'Hey, you're the lead singer for that band back in the sixties?'

The hitcher was not happy at being recognized. 'I'm Alex.'

‘My name is Todd. I thought you looked familiar. Where you headed?’

‘New Orleans.’

‘You won’t believe this. That’s where I’m headed. What part of town do you live in?’

‘I live in the Storyville area.’

‘I’m not familiar with Storyville. I just moved to New Orleans last week.’

‘It’s just north of the French Quarter. I’m guessing you probably know where that is, right?’

Todd missed the sarcasm. ‘Yeh, I should be able to take you all the way. I’m staying in the Lower Garden district. It’s kinda run down but it’s up and coming.’

‘Dude, the LGD is positively yuppified compared to where I live.’

Alex paused then continued.

‘Hey look, I know beggars can’t be choosers, but I have a favor to ask. Can we not talk about my career, especially the early part? That’s all anybody ever wants to talk about. It’s just gotten to be a real drag the last decade or so. I mean can you imagine how Ron Howard feels every time someone calls him Opie. Or how Woody Allen feels when people ask when are you going to make a sequel to ‘Bananas’?’

‘Point made. Point taken.’

‘Don’t get me wrong. I’m grateful for the ride you know.’

'And I'm glad for the company. I wasn't looking forward to this long drive alone. I reckon we can talk about food. I just bought a sack of Krystal's. Want to eat?'

'Actually I am pretty hungry.'

'Got barbecue, too, from Jackson Avenue.'

'Righteous. I'll have to put you in some gas down the road.'

Todd was elated. They were hitting it off.

'Wait, there's more. Got PBR, in quart bottles yet. I bought them last night but they're still cold in the cooler. I kinda overdid it last night. I'm laying off but you help yourself. You know someone once told me that in Alabama they don't even have beer in quarts.'

'Yeah. Been to Muscle Shoals a few times. I used to bring my quarts with me when I'd go down there. Got pulled over once. Spent a long afternoon in an Alabama jail. They were gonna charge me with transporting liquor across state lines but reduced it to simple possession. Just dumb luck that I passed the breathalyzer test. I guess the long wait at the jail helped. They even let me mail them a check for the fine. Good thing that. I was flat broke.'

'The things we do for beer. They had you in a cell?'

'No, I sat in a holding area, but I could see the cells from where I was. The constable was actually a pretty good guy. And I got to know one of the trusties pretty well. But you just naturally know you don't want to spend the night in that place.'

'So did he want to talk about your career? Sorry, you don't have to answer that.'
'I'll answer anyway. He didn't know me from Adam. So are we

picking up another rider? You're packing some pretty serious groceries here.'

'Nope, this was all for me. I don't remember eating since breakfast yesterday. Krystal's are still the world's best hangover food.'

'Amen to that.'

'Plus there's not a lot of barbecue in the Big Easy. I just wanted to take a little Memphis back with me.'

'Oh. Well excuse me if I'm messing that up.'

'Far from it, Alex.'

After a half hour of serious chowing down, the conversation became more relaxed.

'You seem to know your way around Memphis pretty well. Are you a native?' Alex asked.

'With my rural accent and all I'm assuming you just asked that to make conversation. I'm a small town boy. But I've lived in Memphis all my adult life. I went to Memphis State, found a job and stayed. So from the seventies until very recently, I've been a solid citizen of the Bluff City. But you are, right? A Memphis native that is?'

'Yeah. I actually am. Natives are kind of few and far between. Sometimes I think half the population of Memphis is from Mississippi.'

'So what made you decide to leave for New Orleans?'
'Well we kind of touched on it already. All anybody in Memphis wanted to talk about was my early career. Down here it's a whole

different world. I mean New Orleans is like a foreign country to begin with. And well, that goes double for my neighborhood. It's full of characters. I blend in with the scenery. Down there I'm just a regular dude leading a regular life. My wife likes that. Most of the music press don't know I live there and those that do are afraid to come into the neighborhood. I've made some good friends there who just dig you for yourself. I guess that sounds a little corny.'

'You know what. I've only been there a week but I kinda know what you're saying. New Orleans people seem real. The ones I've met anyway.'

'So Todd, what made you leave Memphis?'

'It's a long complicated story. I'll make it short and simple for both our sakes. My wife and I split up. I lost my job. Nobody in Memphis would hire me. I found work in New Orleans. I moved. Or I'm in the process of moving I should say.'

'That's pretty short and simple.'

'It's what I do.'

'Come again?'

'I'm a computer nerd. I get paid to take something long and complicated and make it short and simple. It's called deconstruction. For some reason it pisses people off. I'm pretty good at it though.'

'Yeah, I reckon you are. Sorry about you and your old lady.'

'No big deal. As BB says the thrill was gone. That was 6 months ago. Ancient history. Right now I'm just trying to look ahead. I'm finding that it's easier said than done.'

‘Yeah, tell me about it.’

‘I have a lot of good memories about Memphis, especially the seventies. Overton Park, the Highland Hashbury, concerts at the Shell. My ex and I met at the Shell. I remember once there was this group at the Shell called Trapeze. They recorded the concert and ended up releasing it as a live album. The album cover was a shot of the audience. We all would go to Poplar Tunes and try to find ourselves and people we knew on the cover. Some of us even bought the album. Memphis in the seventies was something special. I always wondered about the sixties though. What were the sixties like in Memphis?’

Alex gave it some thought.

‘Well first of all you need to understand, Memphis is ten years behind the rest of the country. In Memphis the seventies were the sixties. But the actual sixties were cool enough. I became a teenager, got my own car and became a millionaire all in the sixties. Midtown as such was not yet happening. Downtown was a ghost town after dark. Beale street was practically a three block long piece of plywood. Back then Poplar was the strip. We used to cruise up and down the strip through all hours of the night. And the Krystal was a place to light for a few minutes. We’d cruise in and out of there to check out the babe situation and then head back out Poplar to the Shoney’s and check out the scene there.’

‘So you were into the music scene by then, did you have any run ins with Elvis?’

‘No. He was way before me. By the time I was making the scene Elvis had become pretty reclusive which is something I now understand by the way. He had pretty much gone Hollywood so to speak. He was in Memphis but not of it if that makes any sense to you.’

‘Yeah it does.’

‘I never was much into Elvis anyway. Please God don’t strike me dead. But then came the Beatles. They changed everything. I had a big stack of 45 records but the first album I ever bought was ‘Meet the Beatles’ which, by the way, I bought at Poplar Tunes. First thing after that I got a guitar and started a band with some school buddies. Oh yeah, me and half of Memphis. And bam, just like that it was the golden age of garage bands, the Counts, the Gentrys, the Guilloteens and a hundred other lesser imitators. We had all the babes. You didn’t even have to be any good as long as you had Beatle hair and looked cool playing a guitar. There was at last a way for non jocks to score some female attention.’

Alex was on a roll. He grabbed another quart.

‘Then there were teen clubs cropping up all over Memphis to accommodate all the aspiring groups and uh, groupies. When we weren’t cruising Poplar, we’d hit the clubs. My favorite was the Teen Tango on Madison. I used to go there to check out who was up and coming. Every week they would have a battle of the bands. You remember Battle of the Bands, right? After the bands finished playing, the audience would vote on who was the best.’

Todd laughed, ‘Yeah, I used to know this guy who called them battlin’ of the bands.’

‘Yeah well, the house band at Teen Tango was the Cheshire Cats. They owned the place so to speak. They would take on all comers and they always homered the competition big time. They even beat the Gentrys by some ridiculous count like a hundred votes to eight.’

He paused a moment.

‘It’s funny how things you don’t think much about at the time end up staying with you. But one night there’s this band from out-of-town called the Spyders, and they’re going to battle The Cheshire fuckin’ Cats. And were they weird? I mean they’re dressed in black from head to toe. Literally! They’re wearing these black masks. They look like professional wrestlers or something. I half expected Lance Russell to introduce them. And they’re trying to be cool about it. But even wearing those masks you can tell that they’re a bunch of scared, skinny small town boys. All except the drummer.’

‘The drummer wasn’t scared?’

‘No, the drummer wasn’t skinny.

‘So the Cheshire Cats, as always, are dressed to the nines in their pinstripe blazers. And they got their Beatle hair going complete with peroxided bangs. They’re like the epitome of Memphis high school frat cats. They go on first and they’re going through all these histrionics. And the bass and the guitar players are all trying to see who can play the most notes. And of course the home crowd is digging it. They always did put on a helluva good visual show.’

Alex paused for effect.

‘Then the Spyders get up there. And you’re feeling for them before they even begin to play. To begin with they have practically no equipment. They have two amps, a Supro and a Fender, for three guitars and two mikes. You wonder how they have the nerve to even get up there. The energy is just weird and unsettling. I almost left. Then they start to play. They open with something like Latin Lupe Lu which has a bitchin’ good drum line. And that drummer, he’s big to begin with but he plays even bigger. He controls the whole room: the lead, the rhythm, the bass, hell the audience even. They're all in lock step with that drummer. Tight as a fist. And all that weird energy just comes into focus and there is some of the most intense, angst ridden rock and roll you ever heard coming from that stage. They're scared shitless and pouring it all into the music. That music had a life of its own. I don't think they even realized how good it was. And the amps are strained to the max. I thought that poor Supro was going to explode. Then they do this medley of Bo Diddley songs that goes on for like 10 minutes with the drummer never missing a beat. I've heard groups do that since but they were the first. Then they do some Beatles and Stones that nobody else was covering.

'Well long story short, the Cats won but the voting was close, like sixty something to fifty something. I mean in previous battles the voting had never been anywhere near that close. And were the Cats pissed. Those small town dudes had won over the home crowd. Normally, being from out-of-town, the Spyders would have gotten a good ass kicking out back in the parking lot. But the mean kids dug them too, man.

'I've seen a thousand groups. Sometimes I feel like I've played in a thousand groups. But that night stayed with me. Every time I do 'No Sex', I feel like I'm channeling the Spyders. Never heard of them since. I always wondered what happened to them. Probably driving tractors in Haywood county.'

'Hey, you know I grew up in those parts.'

'No offense. Just telling a story.'

'And a good story it is. But there was lots more going on back then, musically I mean. Stax was pretty well established. American Studios was on the scene. Muscle Shoals was just starting to happen. You were involved in all that weren't you?'

‘Yeah, and that would come under the category of what I don’t want to talk about.’

‘Of course. So, do you come back to Memphis often?’

‘Yeah, every couple of months anyway. I still have contacts and friends there. There’s always some new gig in the offing.’

‘And you always hitch a ride?’

‘Not always. Just sometimes. Got to pay the dues if…. , well, you know how the rest of that goes. Plus normally, it’s a good way to avoid people who know me.‘

‘Oh. Sorry if I messed that up.’

‘Far from it, Todd. So what about you? What brought you back up here? You didn’t get a little homesick did you?’

‘Yeah I guess maybe. I mostly just got stir crazy. There was a lot happening last week. I mean there was a whole butt load of heavy shit happening last week non stop. I was going through some serious changes. And then bam, it was the weekend and I had all this time, all this quiet. This girl I met tells me she has to go back to Atlanta for a few days on business. She’s probably hooking up with her back home stud muffin in the process. The walls were closing in on me so I just jumped in the car Saturday afternoon and next thing I know I’m on Lamar Avenue surrounded by 18 wheelers.

‘It’s literally been a weird trip. I didn’t call or drop in on anyone. I just grabbed a quart and rode around all night. I checked out all the familiar haunts. I never even got out of the car. I guess I was afraid I might run into my ex. But mainly nothing looked the same. I felt like a stranger, like I didn’t belong anymore, like I was behind a glass wall. It was just plumb weird. At one point I actually drove out to Memphis State and checked out the old dorm just to see what it was like. I was dying to pee and figured I might as well do it while I was there. I stopped just short of entering when I realized that it had been changed to a girl's dorm. That was the perfect punctuation to a totally screwed up night.'

'Wow. You know that's pretty high school, dude.'

'Yeah well, Tiger High.'

'You were lucky you didn't get pulled over.'

'Tell me about it. After that little episode I even had a notion to drive all the way back to New Orleans. Luckily I ended up finding a motel.'

'At least you made that good decision. Probably saved your life.'

'Yeah well, today I wake up at noon. I'm hungover like a bear. And I realize there's nothing to do but head back. So I figure while I was up here I might as well get a few things out of storage. That way it wasn't a completely wasted trip.'

'It wasn't a wasted trip, dude. Looks to me like you were just saying good bye. The way Morrison did when he left L. A. for Paris.'

'Say that again?'

'Back in '71, Jim Morrison of the Doors left L. A. for Paris. And the last month before he left, he spent entire days walking the streets of Hollywood. Just looking around, not talking to anyone. He was saying good bye. It was like deep down he knew he would never see L. A. again. That's what you were doing last night.'

‘Maybe so. Thanks for the thought anyway. Morrison’s right about one thing, people are definitely strange when you’re a stranger.’

‘Sure. So, you didn’t see any family? Do you have any family here?’

‘Not really. My mother remarried and is living in New Mexico. I have a few distant cousins scattered all over. None of them are in Memphis. I have one uncle who’s in assisted living out in Collierville. Last month when I looked in on him he didn’t know who I was. Guess it wouldn’t have hurt to at least see how he was doing. I was pretty messed up last night, even without the beer.’

‘I’d say you were. I do know one thing. It’s real easy to make yourself crazy over things in the past. Any fool can do that. I’m telling you, dude. Now that you’ve said good bye, don’t ever look back. Sometimes shit just happens and there’s nothing you could’ve done about it. People in New Orleans know that better than anybody. ’

‘I’m sure you can speak firsthand on that. You were living there when Katrina hit right?’

‘That’s correct.’

‘If you don’t want to talk about it, I’ll understand. I’ve already had a blow by blow from someone who was living in the Ninth Ward.’

‘It’s cool. Storyville was nothing like that bad. We stayed relatively high and dry. We left when the mayor told us to and came back when he said we could. Our neighborhood ended up taking in a lot of people who weren’t as fortunate. That’s it. Short and simple as you say.’

‘I’m glad to hear you came out okay.’

‘Thanks. Say that’s a good looking radio you got. Is it aftermarket?’

‘Yeah, the factory job wouldn’t play homemade CD’s. I had a friend who worked at a detail shop. He sold me the top of the line. Claimed it was the same system he sold to Billy Gibbons when ZZ Top was staying in Memphis. It’s probably worth as much as the car.’

‘Care for some music? I just happen to have a fresh burned CD right here.’

‘Memphis songs?’

‘Yeah, although a lot of them were recorded in Muscle Shoals. But that’s another story. Some are pretty obscure. There’s some old Travis Wammack songs nobody ever knew about. And some New Orleans songs’

‘Cool. Let’s hear it.’

After that the conversation dropped off in favor of music and beer drinking. As the brew took its effect, Alex offered the occasional comment or opinion. He talked at some length about the assassination of Dr. King. How it changed Memphis and its people forever. He pointed out that despite the huge success of the hit song ‘Shaft’, it proved to be a supernova signaling the eventual collapse of Stax records and the whole Memphis music scene in general.

But mostly they just listened to the music.

This took them to the first rest stop. Alex insisted on paying for the gas. Then he explained that he hadn’t slept much the night before and crashed. Todd got a much needed cup of coffee. It was pretty awful; but it was strong. Ronnie's New Orleans coffee had spoiled him. He managed to get it down and zoned out. A long stretch in silence took them to another fill up and rest stop.

As they got closer to New Orleans, Alex stirred and began to talk about family and friends. By early evening they arrived. With some help, Todd navigated the eighteenth century street grid of the neighborhood and got to Alex's house. It looked positively ancient. The wood siding was bare and faded gray. The paint that remained might have been the original coat. It had a magical quality. It even had a huge wisteria vine that completely framed the porch and roof line.

'That's one impressive vine. It looks as old as the house.'

'It was planted by Louis Tiffany over a hundred years ago. He was supposedly a real wisteria freak. He lived in this house for a while. He and Edgar Degas used to hang out here. Or so I'm told. Hey keep the CD.'

The look on Alex's face clearly said that this was his home. Todd looked forward to the day when he would feel that way about his home. They agreed to look each other up sometime though that seemed a remote possibility.

Leaving Alex's house Todd was disoriented. He drove around until he found Claiborne. From there he knew the way back to the Creole Oaks. He unloaded the additional belongings he had brought back from Memphis. Rather than make a fuss of arranging them just so, he simply set them down. By now all that was left of his hangover was a dull headache. His stomach was good and he was ready for a beer. The cooler was empty. Alex had finished off the PBR so he grabbed a Dixie from the small refrigerator.

The late summer sunset was beautiful from his balcony overlooking Melpomene. As he sat and watched, he pondered the events of the previous 24 hours. Was he insane? Was he losing it? Alex had suggested that it wasn't a wasted trip. That it had happened for a reason. Maybe there was something to that. Maybe this hiatus had gotten something out of his system. At any rate, he now realized he couldn't go back even if he wanted to.

He thought about Brandi. The 'woman in his life' was at best a maybe. He thought about his 'sit down' talk with Donny. What might Sal require of him? Indeed he might never be as comfortable or as secure as he had been back in Memphis. But this was home now. He would need to make peace with these facts. He made a mental note to go see Ronnie sometime in the coming week.

He heard the clanging of a streetcar on St. Charles. Looking down through the sprawling branches of the live oaks he could see where he'd parked the hatchback. It needed washing in the worst way. He realized that there are some things that never change. He gave thanks for the constants in his life then took a big swallow of beer. He got up and retrieved his guitar. As he picked out a song on the old Gibson, he thought it had never sounded so good. The sunset became even more beautiful.

Epilogue

Three hundred miles away, the Old Señor sat on the church pew in front of Leland's Sundries watching that same sunset. He was drinking a peach Nehi and chewing forever on a bite of beef jerky. He, Todd, and the setting sun formed the three points of a triangle. He could feel the connection. He could sense that something about today was different. Todd had stayed true to his path. He had found his spot. The elder took another sip from his Nehi and allowed himself to indulge in a moment of gratification.

He could also see a more ultimate reality. Betsy had been the first omen. Katrina had been the second. There would be a third. The levees around the lake, the river, and the canals were being re-secured. But the winds had changed. The water was rising and the land was sinking. The day was coming when the great primordial swamp would reclaim the landscape. This corner of God's green earth would return to its Jurassic splendor.

The Old Señor could see all of this. In the meantime he would endure. He would rise each day with the sun and find his spot. There he would have paradise and lunch. And there he would sit and behold the amazing dance that was taking place before him.

59266315R00133

Made in the USA
Charleston, SC
31 July 2016